BIBLE STORIES

for TEENS

Find Your Identity, Build Unshakable Faith

Live with Confidence

& Follow God's Purpose for Your Life

GRACEFUL GROWTH

Contents

READER BONUS

Start Strong with Your Free Companion Journal

The Faith Journal for Teens is a powerful weekly guide that helps you apply what you learn, grow your confidence, and stay rooted in your identity.

FAITH JOURNAL FOR TEENS

52-WEEK GUIDE TO BUILD CONFIDENCE

DISCOVER YOUR IDENTITY

GROW IN FAITH & MAKE WISE CHOICES THAT LAST

PERFECT COMPANION TO BIBLE STORIES FOR TEENS

GRACEFUL GROWTH

Use it alongside this book to reflect on what God is teaching you.

Step 1: Leave a Quick Review

Loved what you've read so far?
Your review helps others discover this book and supports future
faith-based resources.

<< Scan here to leave a review >>

Step 2: Get Your Free Companion Journal

Go deeper with the *Faith Journal for Teens*— 52-week guide to build
confidence, grow in faith, and reflect on what matters most.

<< Scan to get the book now >>

Introduction

Have you ever felt like you're drowning in expectations, but no one even notices you're struggling? It's like the world is shouting at you to be louder, smarter, prettier, better—while you're just trying to breathe. Maybe it's the grind of school, the weight of expectations, or just trying to seem like you've got it together when, inside, you're feeling anything but strong.

If any of that sounds familiar, take a deep breath—you're not alone. Growing up today is loud, messy, and overwhelming. I've been there too. That's precisely why this book exists.

The Bible might feel super old or out of touch—but dig a little deeper, and you'll find it's packed with real people who struggled with the same things you do: fear, identity, purpose, pressure. They questioned themselves. They made mistakes. They faced impossible situations. But through every single moment, God never let go of them.

This isn't just a collection of Bible stories. It's a guide for *your* life. Each chapter connects ancient truth to today's chaos—things like anxiety, friendship drama, comparison, insecurity, tough choices, and the big questions about who you are and why you matter. Faith isn't about having it all figured out; it's about starting something *real* with God—a relationship that gives you peace when everything's spinning, strength when you feel small, and direction when the path ahead looks blurry.

What makes this book different? It won't give you a lecture. It won't ask you to pretend or perform. Instead, it meets you in the mess with honesty, encouragement, and truth that gets to the heart of where you're coming from.

Inside, you'll meet people who were overlooked, underestimated, and utterly unsure of themselves, just like we all feel sometimes. But God still used them to do incredible things. As you read, I'll help you connect their stories to *your* own and start seeing yourself the way God sees you.

Because you're not just what people say or post about you. You're not defined by your test scores, your followers, or the labels others slap on you. Who you are goes *way* deeper than that—and when your identity is rooted in something unshakable, everything starts to change.

So if you're ready to ditch the pressure and build the kind of confidence that lasts—the kind grounded in truth and faith—then yeah, you're in the right place. This journey won't be perfect, but it will be real. And you won't be walking it alone.

Let's dive in.

Chapter 1

Discovering Your Identity

Do you ever feel like no matter how hard you try, you're still not enough?

Do you find yourself constantly adjusting who you are—toning things down, faking confidence, or hiding parts of yourself—just to be accepted? It's a relentless battle, trying to fit into expectations that never seem to align with your true self. It's as if the world hands you a mold and says, "Be this." But when you don't fit, the unspoken message is: *You're not enough as you are.*

Maybe you've been told, "You should speak up more," or "Why can't you be more like them?"—as if there's a checklist for who you're supposed to be, and somehow, you keep missing the mark. It's as if the world expects you to be a highlight reel instead of a real person.

Maybe you've been called "too quiet" or "too dramatic." You don't play a sport or obsess over trends. Perhaps people have labeled you in ways that made you feel small or invisible.

But here's the truth: God's not looking for the version of you that fits everyone else's expectations. He's after the real you—the one He created on purpose, with purpose.

What if the very things you thought disqualified you—the quirks, the doubts, the stuff you hide—are actually what God values and wants to use? Your uniqueness is not a flaw but a strength waiting to be discovered.

This is where we begin: not with a fake version of who you think you should be but by embarking on a journey of self-discovery. The kind of identity that isn't shaken by opinions, likes, or labels—but grounded in something way deeper. Something unshakable.

***

Samuel: When God Calls Your Name

Have you ever had one of those nights where you're just lying there, staring at the ceiling, wondering what your purpose is? Maybe you've whispered a prayer, asking God to show up, or just sighed, feeling unsure if He's even listening. That's precisely where Samuel was—young, uncertain, and just beginning to understand what it meant to hear from God.

You can find his story in **1 Samuel 3,** but here's the short version with significant meaning.

Samuel's journey didn't begin with a spotlight. He was just a boy living in the temple, serving under the priest Eli. He ran errands. Lit lamps. Cleaned up. He was faithful in quiet ways, day after day. Nobody looked at Samuel and thought, "There goes a future prophet!" He was there. Obedient. Quiet. Willing.

But God saw him.

One night, something unusual happened. As Samuel lay down to sleep, he heard a voice calling him: *"Samuel!"*

Startled, he got up and ran to Eli's room. *"Here I am. Did you call me?"*

Eli said no. It must've been a dream. *"Go back to bed."*

But then it happened again. And again. Finally, Eli realized—it was God's calling. So he told Samuel, "Next time, say, 'Speak, Lord, your servant is listening.'"

So the next time Samuel heard his name, he did just that. He responded with a simple, 'Speak, Lord, your servant is listening.'

That simple response—I'm listening—was the beginning of Samuel's calling. God didn't just speak to him once. He kept speaking. And as Samuel grew, so did his influence. He became one of the greatest prophets in Israel's history. But it all started with a small, quiet moment that looked like nothing special, except it was everything.

And maybe that's exactly what your life looks like right now.

You're not leading a nation. You're not on a big stage. But you might be sitting in your room, wondering if God sees you, hears you, or even wants to use someone like you.

Samuel's story is a powerful reminder that God doesn't look for the most impressive or the most accomplished. He looks for the willing. He looks for you.

He didn't come in fire or thunder. He came in a whisper. And it took Samuel time and help to realize it.

It's not about always feeling spiritual or having all the answers. It's about being open. It's about being attentive. It's about being ready to say, 'God, I'm listening.'

Maybe you've been asking God to speak and wondering why He hasn't. But what if He has been talking—just softly, gently, in the quiet?

He might be calling you to reach out to a friend. To step away from something toxic. To trust Him with the thing that scares you. To dream a little bigger. To believe you matter.

God doesn't look for the loudest voice. He looks for an open heart. Samuel didn't try to impress God. He just showed up, stayed faithful, and said yes. That was enough.

And that's enough for you, too.

Pause & Reflect

- Do you ever feel like God is silent—or like He wouldn't speak to someone like you?

- What would it look like to slow down this week and say, "Speak, Lord—I'm listening"?

One last thing to remember:

God doesn't speak to perfect people. He talks to listening hearts. Don't wait to feel ready—God might be calling your name right now.

***

Esther's Secret – Embracing Your Unique Purpose

You can read Esther's story in the Book of Esther, especially chapters 2–7.

Esther's story didn't begin in a palace. It started with a loss.

She was a young orphan, raised by her older cousin Mordecai in a foreign land where her people—the Jews—were outsiders. No royal pedigree. No glamorous future. Just quiet resilience and a life marked by faith, survival, and deep cultural roots.

But Esther's quiet beginning didn't go unnoticed by God.

One day, a royal decree changed everything. The King of Persia was seeking a new queen, and through a series of events that seemed more like fate than chance, Esther was brought into the palace. Suddenly, she found herself in a world of gold and luxury—but also secrecy and danger.

She had to hide who she truly was to stay safe. Her name, her faith, her people—all concealed.

Yet God hadn't hidden her. He had placed her.

Esther's journey wasn't just about beauty or position—it was about divine purpose. She didn't transform herself to fit in. Instead, she discovered her true self when it mattered most, showing immense courage in the face of danger.

Then came the crisis.

A man named Haman rose to power in the kingdom, and his hatred for the Jews turned into a terrifying plan: wipe them out completely. Esther, now queen, was the only one in a position to stop it. But to do so, she'd have to risk everything. In Persian law, even the queen couldn't approach the king without being summoned—doing so could mean death.

At first, Esther was terrified. Who wouldn't be?

But then came Mordecai's words, which still echo today: **"Who knows but that you have come to your royal position for such a time as this?"** (Esther 4:14)

Esther's fear didn't paralyze her. Instead, it was her unwavering faith that propelled her forward, inspiring hope and empowerment in the face of adversity.

She asked her people to fast and pray. She took time to prepare—not just outwardly, but inwardly. Her courage didn't come from confidence in herself. It came from trust in the God who had placed her right where she was.

Then, wearing her royal robes and carrying quiet resolve, Esther entered the throne room.

And the king welcomed her.

She didn't rush into a dramatic plea. She waited. She hosted a banquet. She created space for trust. And at just the right moment, Esther revealed the truth, risking everything to stand up for her people.

Her voice changed history.

Because of Esther, the plot was exposed, the Jews were saved, and a day that was meant for mourning became a celebration still remembered today—**Purim.**

Esther didn't save her people by force. She didn't shout. She didn't lead an army. She used her position, her words, and her God-given courage.

And here's the part that speaks to us: Esther didn't feel ready. She wasn't fearless. But she showed up.

She reminds us that bravery isn't about having no fear—it's about moving forward despite it. You don't have to be loud to be brave. You don't need a title to make an impact. And you don't have to feel powerful to be chosen.

You may have been wondering about your purpose. You may feel your voice doesn't matter. But just like Esther, you've been placed in this moment, in this time, on purpose.

The question isn't, "Am I enough?"

The real question is, "Am I willing?"

Because God doesn't call the fearless, He calls the faithful.

Pause & Reflect

- Have you ever felt like you needed to hide who you truly are to be accepted?

- What would it look like to trust that God placed you right where you are for a reason?

One last thing to remember:

You don't need to be fearless to make a difference. You need to say yes—even if your voice shakes.

***

Joseph's Coat: Standing Out Without Fear

Joseph stood out—and not always in ways that felt good.

He was the youngest for a while—the dreamer. The one who always seemed a little *too confident* for his good—or at least, that's how his older brothers saw it.

You can read Joseph's full story in **Genesis 37–50**, and trust me—it's a rollercoaster. It begins with a gift: a special coat that his father, Jacob, gave him. It wasn't just colorful. It was bold, vibrant, and meaningful—a symbol that Joseph was cherished. But instead of making life better, it made him a target. His brothers saw the coat not as a sign of love but as favoritism. And they hated him for it.

Then Joseph started having dreams—big, strange ones. Dreams in where others bowed down to him. He probably didn't mean to sound proud when he shared them. Maybe he didn't know how to hold something that big quietly. But his brothers heard those dreams and saw a threat.

Their anger boiled over. One day, in a field far from home, they stripped off Joseph's coat, threw him into a pit, and sold him into slavery.

Here's the hard, beautiful truth: they took his coat—but they *couldn't take his calling*.

Joseph's journey from that moment wasn't smooth. He was betrayed, falsely accused, thrown into prison, and forgotten. But through every twist, Joseph didn't lose who he was. He held onto his identity—not in the coat, not in the approval of others, but in who God had always said he was.

In the dark places, Joseph continued to use his gifts. He interpreted dreams. He worked with integrity. He honored God. Eventually, he rose from prisoner to Pharaoh's right hand—a position of incredible influence and impact.

But what makes Joseph's story unforgettable isn't the comeback. It's what he did when the very brothers who betrayed him showed up again, desperate and starving.

He didn't lash out. He didn't seek revenge.

He forgave. He wept. He told them, *"You meant to harm me, but God intended it for good, to accomplish what is now being done, the saving of many lives"* (**Genesis 50:20**, NIV).

That's not a weakness. That's unshakable strength—the kind that comes from knowing who you are, even when life has tried to rewrite your identity.

So if you've ever felt misunderstood, if your uniqueness made you a target, or if people have tried to define you by your worst moments, Joseph's story is your reminder: **they don't get the final say.**

God knows the whole story. He sees what's been taken, what's been twisted, what's been used against you—and still, He's not finished.

Standing out can feel lonely. But you weren't made to blend in. You were made to carry something bright. Something bold. Something that reflects the God who never stops writing redemption into broken chapters.

So if your "coat" feels like too much, too loud, too different, too exposed—wear it anyway, not in pride, but in purpose.

You are seen. You are chosen. And your story? It's far from over.

Pause & Reflect

- Have you ever felt like you had to shrink to make others comfortable?

- What gifts or qualities has God given you that you've been afraid to own?

One last thing to remember:

They may try to strip the coat, but they can't steal the calling.

Leah's Journey: When You're Tired of Feeling Second Best

Genesis 29–30

Leah's story doesn't begin with a spotlight—it starts in the shadow of someone else's beauty.

In a world where appearance seemed to define value, Leah, a woman of her time, was often compared to her younger sister, Rachel. The Bible tells us Rachel was stunning—*"beautiful in form and appearance"* (Genesis 29:17)—while Leah had "weak" or "tender" eyes, a description that left her feeling less-than, overlooked, and unloved.

Maybe you've felt that too.

Not good enough. Not the first choice. Always compared.

That's where Leah's story begins.

The Marriage No One Cheered For

Leah's father, Laban, tricked Jacob into marrying her. Jacob had worked seven years to marry Rachel, the woman he loved. But on the wedding night, Laban secretly sent Leah instead.

Imagine waking up next to someone who didn't choose you. Imagine starting a marriage with rejection baked in.

Jacob was furious. He still married Rachel a week later, and loved her more. From the very beginning, Leah was in a relationship where she felt invisible.

But God saw her.

When God Sees What Others Miss

The Bible says, *"When the Lord saw that Leah was not loved, he enabled her to conceive..."* (Genesis 29:31). Leah began to have sons, each named after a cry of her heart:

- **Reuben**: *"The Lord has seen my misery. Surely, my husband will love me now."*

- **Simeon**: *"Because the Lord heard that I am not loved..."*

- **Levi**: *"Now, at last, my husband will become attached to me..."*

She was trying so hard—using motherhood, loyalty, anything—to win the love she desperately wanted.

But something shifted.

When her fourth son was born, she said something different:

- **Judah**: *"This time, I will praise the Lord."*

Leah's transformation is a powerful testament to the hope that lies in turning our hearts towards God. In that moment, something powerful happened—Leah, the girl who felt unwanted and unseen, became the mother of a lineage that would lead to **Jesus**.

Yes, **Judah**, the son she bore when she finally stopped striving and started praising, became the ancestor of Christ.

What Leah's Story Tells Us

You don't have to be the most popular, the most followed, or the most praised to be chosen by God.

God doesn't rank us by our appearance, status, or who notices us. He looks at the heart. And sometimes, it's the ones the world overlooks that He uses in the most powerful ways.

Maybe you've felt like Leah.

You try and try, but still feel second best. You wonder if anyone sees how hard you're trying. You're tired of competing, comparing, or pretending to be someone you're not just to be loved.

Leah's story reminds us:

- God sees your pain.

- He hears your cries.

- He values you deeply, before you make any changes.

Your worth isn't found in someone else's opinion. It's found in the God who created you on purpose.

Remember, your worth isn't found in someone else's opinion. It's found in the God who created you on purpose. And sometimes, your most incredible breakthrough comes the moment you stop chasing love—and start resting in the love God already gives.

Pause & Reflect

- Have you ever felt second best, like someone else always shines brighter?

- What are you hoping will make you feel "enough," and could you lay that down before God?

- How might your story change if you believed, deep down, that God sees and chooses you right now?

One last thing to remember:

You don't have to fight for your place in someone else's heart. You already have one in God's. And like Leah, your story might be shaping a legacy you don't even see yet.

***

Hagar – The God Who Sees You

Read her story in Genesis 16 and Genesis 21:8–21

Have you ever felt invisible, like no one notices what you're going through or how much you're carrying? Hagar gets it. Her story isn't one most people talk about.

Still, it holds deep power, especially when you're wrestling with questions of identity, belonging, or feeling unseen.

Hagar was a servant—a woman with little to no power, status, or voice. She worked for Sarah, the wife of Abraham, and had little say over her own life. One day, Sarah made a painful decision. She couldn't have children, so she told Abraham to have a child with Hagar instead. At that time and in that culture, Hagar had no choice but to flee. She became pregnant, and suddenly, things got even worse.

Sarah treated her harshly, and Hagar could no longer take it. She ran away into the desert, pregnant and alone, not knowing where to go.

And that's where something extraordinary happened.

In Genesis 16, an angel of the Lord found Hagar in the wilderness. He called her by name—**Hagar**. This act of recognition was profound. No one in the story had bothered to treat her like a person, let alone speak to her with care. But God did, showing a deep understanding of her plight.

The angel didn't just offer comfort—he gave her a promise: her son would grow into a great nation. He gave her direction, hope, and a sense of identity. And in that moment, Hagar said something no one had ever said before in Scripture.

She gave God a name: **"El Roi,"** which means "The God who sees me."

Can you imagine the depth of that moment? After being treated like she didn't matter, she was finally seen. Not as a servant. Not a problem. But as a person valued and known by God. This transformation in her self-perception is a powerful reminder of our worth.

Later, after Isaac (Sarah's child) was born, Hagar was sent away again—this time with her son, Ishmael. They wandered in the desert with nothing left. Hagar believed they were going to die.

But once again, God showed up.

He provided water in the wilderness and repeated His promise. Hagar and her son would not be forgotten. God had a plan for them. And once again, she realized she was never alone. This constant presence of God is a source of reassurance for all of us.

Hagar's story is raw and honest. She didn't have control over her life. She was mistreated, misunderstood, and overlooked. But her story proves something incredible:

God doesn't overlook the overlooked. He sees the one no one else sees.

You may feel like others don't get what you're going through. Like your pain, your story, or your feelings don't matter. But the God of the universe sees you, just like He saw Hagar.

He knows your name. He hears your cries. And He has not forgotten you.

You don't need to have status, popularity, or a perfect story to be important to God. Hagar didn't. And yet, God showed up just for her. That means He'll show up for you, too.

Pause & Reflect

- Have you ever felt unseen or unheard, like you didn't matter?

- What difference would it make to believe that God sees you and cares about your story?

One last thing to remember:

You are not invisible to God. He sees you, He knows your name, and He's walking with you—even in the wilderness.

***

Moses' Stutter: Embracing Imperfections

Moses wasn't the obvious choice.

Not to lead a nation. Not to confront a king. Not to stand at the center of one of the most essential rescue missions in the Bible.

And Moses knew it.

You can read his story in **Exodus 3–4**, where God speaks to him through a burning bush. It's one of the most famous moments in Scripture—but it doesn't begin with confidence. It starts with insecurity.

When God called him, Moses didn't puff up with excitement or shout, "Let's go!" He shrank back. "Who am I to do this?" he asked. "I'm not good with words." Moses stuttered. He doubted. He feared being misunderstood. And in that moment, his flaws felt bigger than the call.

Can you picture it? Alone in the wilderness. The glow of fire on his face. Standing barefoot on holy ground. His heart was pounding. Maybe he looked down at his hands, shaking. Perhaps he wanted to say yes, but his fears screamed out a resounding no.

Have you ever felt that way?

Not smart enough. Not talented enough. Not confident enough. That whisper of "I'm not the right person" echoing in your head?

Here's what's beautiful: God didn't dismiss Moses's fear. He didn't shame him or say, "Just get over it." Instead, God spoke softly, **"I will be with you."**

He didn't ask Moses to be impressive—He just asked him to trust.

And even when Moses still struggled, God gave him support—his brother Aaron—to speak alongside him. That wasn't a punishment. It was grace. A reminder that needing help doesn't make you weak. It makes you human.

Step by step, Moses moved forward. He didn't become a leader overnight. He hesitated. He questioned. He stumbled. But still, he obeyed.

And over time, this man who once begged not to be chosen became the one who lifted his staff as God split the sea, stood before Pharaoh, called down miracles, and led a nation out of slavery.

Not because he was fearless. But because he kept showing up, even with shaking hands and a trembling voice.

Moses' story isn't about perfection. It's about **faithful obedience in the face of fear.** It's about saying yes when your voice shakes. It's about learning to trust that your **weakest parts** might be the exact places where God wants to show up and shine through.

So if you've ever felt like your flaws are too loud, if you've held back because of fear, if you've wondered whether God could use someone like you, remember this:

God doesn't call the flawless.

He calls the willing.

He calls the faithful.

He calls the real you.

You don't need a polished voice or a perfect résumé. You need a heart that says, **"I'll trust You anyway."**

So take the next step—even if it's shaky, even if you stutter, even if you're scared. God isn't asking you to impress Him.

He's asking you to trust Him.

Pause & Reflect

- What flaw or fear has made you feel like you're not enough?

- What would change if you believed God could work through it instead of around it?

One last thing to remember:

God doesn't need you to speak perfectly—to say yes.

What Does This All Mean for You?

You've just walked through six powerful stories. Not of perfect people, but of real people—messy, unsure, often overlooked—who were still seen, still chosen, and still used by God.

- Samuel was just a kid when he first heard God's voice, but he listened and followed.

- Esther didn't start boldly, but her faith gave her the courage and purpose she needed.

- Joseph was betrayed and forgotten, but God turned his pain into purpose.

- Leah lived in the shadow of rejection, yet God saw her and honored her sincerely.

- Hagar felt alone and discarded, but God met her in the wilderness and called her by name.

- Moses—stumbling, doubting, and unsure—became the one who led a nation toward freedom.

These aren't just Bible stories. They're mirrors. They show us what's possible. They remind us what's true. They invite us to believe that the same God who called them calls you, too.

God isn't looking for someone who has it all figured out. He's not waiting for you to become perfect, polished, or popular. He's looking for someone **willing**. Someone open to trying. Someone ready to trust—even when they're still unsure.

That's where you are right now. Still figuring out who you are, what you believe, and where you fit. That's okay. That's exactly where God meets you.

This journey isn't about having all the answers. It's about showing up. It's about becoming.

Every honest question you ask, every quiet prayer you whisper, every moment you choose faith over fear—it all matters. Nothing is wasted. Not the hard days, not the confusion, not even the setbacks.

You don't need to fit someone else's mold. You don't have to pretend you've got it all together.

God delights in who He made you to be—your quiet strength, your hidden talents, your weird sense of humor, your doubts, your dreams, even the messy parts. Especially the messy parts.

So take a breath.

You're already on the path.

If you're wondering what's next, don't stress. Just keep leaning in. Keep looking for God in the stories, in the silence, in your questions, and even in the struggle.

That's where your identity is shaped—not by pressure or performance, but by love.

Let's keep walking this together.

Pause & Reflect

- Which story spoke to you the most, and why do you think that is?

- What part of your story do you think God is still writing?

One last thing to remember:

You don't have to be perfect to start—you have to be willing to take the next step.

Looking Ahead: When Life Gets Hard

The stories in Chapter 1 showed us something powerful:

- God sees you—even when you feel invisible.

- He chooses you—even when you feel unworthy.

- He uses you—even when life feels messy.

But let's be honest—being seen and chosen doesn't make everything easy.

Sometimes, life still hits hard.

Some moments leave you confused, overwhelmed, or straight-up exhausted.

Moments when faith feels like more of a fight than a comfort.

That's precisely where we're heading next.

In Chapter 2, you'll meet people who, just like you, walked through pain, pressure, and adversity. And somehow, with God, they not only survived but thrived.

- Job faced an unimaginable loss.

- Daniel stood firm when everything was stacked against him.

- Jonah ran from his calling.

- Nehemiah rebuilt from ruins.

- Paul kept going through the pain.

- Elijah broke down after a victory.

They were not perfect, and that's OK. They were real, just like you and me.

All of them were real.

And just as He never gave up on them, He will never give up on you.

If you've ever felt like things are falling apart.

If you're tired of pretending you're OK.

If you've been wondering where God is in the middle of your hardest days.

You're not alone.

And you're not forgotten.

Chapter 2 is where we get honest about the struggle. And discover how to walk through it with courage, faith, and hope that holds steady even when life doesn't.

So take a breath.

Let your guard down.

We're going deeper—and it's going to be worth it.

Navigating Challenges and Overcoming Adversity

Job's Story: Holding On When Everything Falls Apart

Imagine waking up one morning to find that everything you held dear was gone. Your family. Your home. Your sense of safety and stability was shattered in an instant.

It sounds like the opening to a heartbreaking novel. But for Job, it was real.

You can find his story in the **Book of Job, chapters 1–42**. Job was a man of deep faith, someone who had it all—wealth, respect, family, and health. And then, one by one, all of it disappeared. Disaster came like a tidal wave: his children were gone, his possessions destroyed, and his body covered in painful sores. He was left sitting in ashes, scraping his wounds with broken pottery.

It would've made sense for him to give up. To grow bitter. To walk away from God.

But Job's first response? Worship.

He whispered, *"The Lord gave, and the Lord has taken away; blessed be the name of the Lord"* (**Job 1:21**, ESV).

That kind of faith doesn't come from pretending everything's fine. It comes from **trusting God even when nothing makes sense**. It stems from heartbreak and the decision to believe that God is still near.

But Job's story isn't all instant faith and peace. He grieved. He cried. He wrestled with long nights and honest questions. And he didn't do it alone—at least not at first.

His friends came and sat beside him in silence. At first, their presence was a gift. Sometimes, just being there matters most.

However, when they began speaking, things got messy. Instead of comforting Job, they started blaming him. Telling him he must've done something wrong to deserve this suffering, and trying to explain his pain away. And that only made it worse.

Have you ever been there? Already hurting—and someone adds judgment instead of compassion?

That kind of pain runs deep.

But Job didn't shut down. He stayed true to his friends, his hurt, and his faith in God. He didn't pretend. He didn't fake smiles or hide his questions. And that honesty? It mattered.

Eventually, God responded. Not with simple answers. Not with explanations that tied everything up neatly. But through a whirlwind, God reminded Job of something greater—the wonder of creation, the depth of mystery, the presence of a God who sees more than we ever could.

In the end, Job's life was restored—his health, his relationships, his home. But the biggest restoration happened inside him. His trust in God deepened. His heart grew quieter, stronger, and more anchored.

Because when everything falls apart, what holds you together is never how much you know—it's *who you trust*.

So if you're walking through something heavy—grief, rejection, confusion—Job's story is for you.

You don't have to pretend to be OK. You don't need perfect answers.

You need to hold on.

Even in your questions. Even in your tears.

You are not forgotten.

God sees you. God hears you.

And even when everything feels uncertain, He is still holding you.

Pause & Reflect

- Have you ever felt like your world was falling apart? What helped you hold on?

- Are there any questions or pains you've been afraid to bring to God?

One last thing to remember:

You don't have to understand everything to trust the One who does.

***

Daniel in the Lion's Den: Courage Under Pressure

Picture a kingdom buzzing with power, politics, and pressure.

Daniel, a foreigner in Babylon, had risen to one of the highest positions in the government. His wisdom, his integrity, and his deep, unshakable faith made him stand out. He wasn't flashy. He wasn't power-hungry. He was just faithful—and *that* made him powerful.

But not everyone admired him.

Jealous officials watched his every move. They couldn't find fault in his work, so they attacked something else—his relationship with God. They knew he wouldn't compromise that.

You can read his story in **Daniel 6**, one of the most powerful portraits of quiet courage in the Bible.

These officials tricked King Darius into passing a law: for thirty days, no one could pray to anyone except the king. Anyone who broke that law would be thrown into a den of lions.

It was a trap—and Daniel knew it.

He also knew what he had to do.

He didn't panic. He didn't rage. He didn't try to hide.

He walked into his room, opened his window—just like he always did—and knelt to pray.

His courage wasn't loud. It wasn't performative.

It was consistent. Steady. Quiet.

Daniel chose to remain faithful, even when he knew it could cost him everything.

The officials caught him, of course. And the punishment was brutal: the lion's den. Imagine that moment—being lowered into the darkness. The sound of growls. The cold floor beneath him. The heavy stone slid into place, sealing him in.

Daniel didn't know what the night would bring. But he did understand *who* was with him.

That was enough.

God sent an angel to shut the mouths of the lions. When morning came, Daniel was alive. Not a scratch on him.

King Darius had stayed up all night, worried for him. At dawn, he ran to the den and cried out, "*Daniel, servant of the living God, has your God rescued you?*"

And from the shadows, Daniel's voice answered: "Yes."

He wasn't just alive—he was whole. And because of Daniel's quiet faith, the king declared across the empire that Daniel's God was the living God—powerful, trustworthy, and worthy of praise.

This isn't just a survival story. It's a story about **staying true to who you are**, even when the pressure is suffocating.

Maybe you've felt that kind of pressure, too—the pressure to blend in, to stay silent about your faith, to change just enough so you don't stand out.

But here's what Daniel shows us:

You don't have to roar to be brave.

You don't have to fight back with noise.

Sometimes, the strongest thing you can do is *kneel*—and stay consistent.

Faith doesn't erase fear.

It gives you something more substantial to hold onto when fear tries to take over.

So when life feels like a lion's den—when you're surrounded by anxiety, expectations, or people who don't understand your values—remember Daniel.

You don't have to compromise to survive. You don't have to hide to belong.

Stay rooted. Stay steady.

And let God meet you in the den.

Pause & Reflect

- Is there a part of your faith or identity you've been tempted to hide?

- What does quiet courage look like in your life right now?

One last thing to remember:

You don't have to roar to be brave—sometimes, you have to kneel.

***

Jonah's Journey: Learning from Mistakes

Have you ever tried to avoid something you *knew* you were meant to do?

Jonah did. Big time.

God asked him to go to Nineveh—a massive city full of people who had utterly lost their way. But for Jonah, it wasn't just a challenging mission. It was *personal*. He didn't think they deserved grace. He didn't want them to get a second chance.

So, instead of following God's call, Jonah ran in the opposite direction. Literally.

He boarded a ship to **Tarshish**, trying to outrun the uncomfortable truth pulling at his heart.

You can read his story in the **Book of Jonah, chapters 1–4**. It's only four chapters, but it's full of big questions about calling, compassion, and change.

Here's the thing: you can't outrun God. Not really.

A violent storm slammed into the ship. The sailors were terrified. They each cried out to their gods, but nothing changed. Finally, they found Jonah below deck and begged him for answers. Jonah knew. He admitted he was running from God. And in a moment of honest surrender, he told them to throw him overboard.

That wasn't a defeat—it was his first step toward owning what he had tried to avoid.

As Jonah sank beneath the waves, swallowed by chaos and consequence, something even more unexpected happened: God provided a way forward.

A great fish swallowed him whole.

For **three long days and nights**, Jonah sat in the dark. Alone. Still. No distractions. No escape. And finally, he did the one thing he had been avoiding—he prayed. Not just for rescue. But for *change*. For mercy. For a chance to begin again.

And God heard him.

The fish spit Jonah out onto dry land. That moment wasn't just a rescue; it was a miracle.

It was *grace*—a second chance.

This time, Jonah listened. He went to Nineveh and delivered God's message. And to his shock, the people listened. They *repented*. They changed. And God, full of mercy, forgave them.

But Jonah? He still struggled.

He sat outside the city, frustrated. How could God forgive people who had done *so much* wrong?

And that's when God gently reminded him of something more profound.

God provided a plant to shade Jonah. Then, the next day, He took it away. Jonah was angry. And God said, **"You're upset about a plant. Shouldn't I care about people?"**

Jonah's story isn't just about running.

It's about *growing*.

It's about learning that God's love isn't based on who we think deserves it.

It's wider. Deeper. More generous than we could ever imagine.

And it's about realizing this: your calling doesn't get canceled because you got off track.

Perhaps you've been running, too.

Not to a ship—but maybe from an apology you don't want to make. A conversation that feels too vulnerable. A decision that takes more faith than you're ready for. Perhaps you've been distracting yourself, putting off something you know you're meant to do.

But here's the truth: **God hasn't given up on you.**

He meets you in the storm. He sits with you in the dark. He's not looking for perfect. He's looking for *willing*.

Healing doesn't begin when life is all cleaned up.

It begins when you *stop running* and you turn around. When you say, "OK, God. I'm ready."

You don't have to be flawless to start over.

You have to stop running.

Pause & Reflect

- Is there something you've been avoiding—out of fear, pride, or uncertainty?

- What would it look like to stop running and take one small step toward growth?

One last thing to remember:

You don't need to be perfect to begin again—just honest enough to turn around.

***

Nehemiah's Walls: Rebuilding After a Setback

Imagine a city with no walls—wide open, vulnerable, and exposed. That was Jerusalem after years of destruction. Once a place of strength and identity, it now lay broken and forgotten.

Sometimes, that's how life feels after a setback.

Like when trust is shattered. Or confidence crumbles. Or something you believed in suddenly falls apart.

You feel unprotected. Unsure. Discouraged.

That's what Nehemiah felt when he heard about his hometown. He was living far away, working as a cupbearer to King Artaxerxes of Persia. He had status, safety, and a decent life—but when the news about Jerusalem's condition reached him, his heart broke.

You can find his story in **Nehemiah, chapters 1–6**, and it's one of the most inspiring accounts of leadership, perseverance, and faith in the Bible.

Nehemiah didn't rush to fix things right away. First, he wept. Then he prayed. He fasted. He brought his heartbreak and questions to God before he ever made a move.

Then, he took action with courage and wisdom.

He went to the king and asked for permission to rebuild Jerusalem's walls. Not only did the king say yes, but he also gave Nehemiah letters of support, resources, and everything he would need to begin again.

Nehemiah returned to a broken city, but he carried a clear vision and a deep sense of purpose.

And he didn't try to do it alone.

He gathered the people. Divided up the work and assigned different sections of the wall to families and teams. *Everyone* had a role. *Everyone* had a reason to fight for what they were building.

But rebuilding wasn't easy.

Enemies mocked them. Threatened them. They tried to sabotage the work. Fear crept in. Fatigue set in. And conflict even stirred within the community itself.

But Nehemiah didn't walk away. He didn't let fear win.

He stayed rooted in prayer. He made adjustments. He spoke with honesty. He led with integrity. And he reminded everyone that this wall wasn't just about bricks and stones—it was about identity, belonging, and hope.

Day by day. Stone by stone. The wall rose.

And when it was finally finished, something *even more powerful* had been restored: **the people's faith.**

They gathered together. They read the Scriptures. They wept with gratitude. What had been broken wasn't just the city walls—it was their sense of who they were. And through this process, which was rebuilt as well.

Nehemiah's story isn't just about architecture.

It's about *healing*.

It's about responding to disappointment without shutting down.

It's about moving forward, even when you're tired, even when others doubt you, even when it feels like too much to handle.

If something in your life feels broken right now—your confidence, your friendships, your sense of purpose—*this story is for you.*

Because what's broken doesn't mean you're finished.

What's cracked doesn't mean you're done.

Things can be rebuilt. And you don't have to do it alone.

Start with prayer.

Gather your people.

Take one small step at a time.

And don't give up when resistance shows up.

You are not beyond repair. You are not too far gone.

Like Nehemiah, you can rise again—with purpose in your heart and faith in your hands.

Pause & Reflect

- What part of your life feels broken or needs rebuilding right now?

- Who can you invite to help you heal, grow, and move forward?

One last thing to remember:

Healing doesn't have to happen all at once—just one faithful step at a time.

***

Paul's Perseverance: Transforming Trials into Triumphs

Paul's life was anything but easy.

He was shipwrecked. Beaten. Imprisoned. Rejected. Chased out of cities. Betrayed and left for dead. And yet, he never gave up.

Before all of that, Paul was known as **Saul**, a man who persecuted Christians with zeal. But everything changed when he encountered Jesus on the road to Damascus. That moment turned his world upside down—not just his beliefs but his *entire purpose*.

You can find pieces of Paul's story throughout the **Book of Acts (chapters 8–28)** and in the New Testament letters he wrote to the early churches.

From the moment he met Jesus, Paul became a tireless messenger of the gospel. He set out on missionary journeys across the ancient world, carrying hope wherever he went—and facing every kind of hardship along the way.

Imagine being shipwrecked in the cold, tossed into crashing waves, clinging to pieces of broken wood in the dark sea. Picture sitting in a dim prison cell—your feet shackled, your back bruised, your body aching—and still choosing to write.

There's no comfort. No applause. Just a flickering oil lamp, a worn scroll, and a man who knows who he is.

Paul's letters, written during his darkest moments, weren't just words of encouragement. They were acts of hope. Of faith. Of worship in the dark.

Even in chains, he kept going.

To the **Philippians**, he wrote, "*Rejoice in the Lord always*"—*while under house arrest.*

To the **Corinthians**, he wrote, "*God's power is made perfect in weakness,*" *while struggling with physical suffering.*

To **Timothy**, a young leader, he wrote, "*Fight the good fight of faith*"—*as his own life neared its end.*

Paul didn't pretend things were easy. He was honest about the pain. But he kept showing up—anchored in purpose, fueled by something more substantial than fear.

His resilience didn't come from being tough.

It came from being **clear** about why he was here.

Paul knew his mission, and it ignited a fire inside him that couldn't be extinguished by hardship.

And the result?

Massive.

Churches were planted. Communities transformed. Lives changed. Generations inspired.

All because one man refused to let pain stop him from living out his calling. Perhaps your challenges don't look like shipwrecks or prison cells. They may look like rejection from people you trusted.

Anxiety that creeps in at night.

Loneliness in a crowded room.

Failure that echoes louder than your accomplishments.

Whatever your storm looks like, Paul's story reminds you that **what feels like defeat might be the beginning of something powerful**.

You don't have to have it all together. You don't need perfect faith or constant strength.

But you *do* need a mission.

Something you believe in.

Something that lights you up.

Something worth getting back up for when life knocks you down.

Find that. Name it. Hold it close.

And when trials come—and they *will*—let that purpose be the reason you keep going.

You don't have to be flawless.

You have to be *faithful*.

One step. One choice. One prayer at a time.

Pause & Reflect

- What challenge or hardship has made you question your purpose?

- What's one thing you feel called to do—even if it scares you a little?

One last thing to remember:

Perseverance isn't about perfection—it's about refusing to quit.

Elijah's Escape: Finding Peace Amidst Chaos

Elijah was a prophet—a man who spoke boldly about God when no one else would.

Just before this moment, he had experienced a literal mountaintop high. You can read his story in **1 Kings 18–19**, where he stood on **Mount Carmel**, called down fire from heaven, and witnessed a miracle that proved God's power in front of an entire nation.

It was a victory—a moment of public success and profound spiritual clarity.

But right after that, everything fell apart.

When Queen Jezebel heard about what happened, she didn't repent. She got angry and threatened Elijah's life. And just like that, the man who had stood so boldly on the mountain was suddenly running for his life.

But Elijah wasn't just running from Jezebel. He was running from pressure. From fear. From the heavy, invisible weight of feeling like *everything was too much.*

He collapsed under a broom tree in the wilderness and whispered one of the most honest prayers in the Bible:
"I've had enough, Lord."

Maybe you've felt that too.

When you're doing all the "right" things but still feel like you're falling apart.

When success doesn't quiet the anxiety.

When you're exhausted from being strong for everyone else.

Here's what's incredible: God didn't rebuke Elijah for breaking down.

Instead, He responded with compassion.

While Elijah slept, an angel came *twice* to offer fresh bread and water. No lectures. No guilt. Just care. Just presence.

Because sometimes, what we need isn't motivation or advice.

Sometimes, we need rest. And God knows that.

Elijah eventually traveled to **Mount Horeb**—a place rich in spiritual history—and found a cave in which to hide. He was alone. Disoriented.

Then God came to meet him.

But not in fire.

Not in the wind.

Not in an earthquake.

God came in a **gentle whisper**.

It was His way of saying, *'I'm not just in the big, miraculous moments.'* I'm here in the quiet, too.

That whisper was enough to begin Elijah's healing.

God reminded him of his purpose. He gave him the next step. He let Elijah know that he wasn't alone—that there were *thousands* of others still standing for truth, even when Elijah felt like the last one left.

Maybe you're in that space too. Perhaps you're doing everything right on the outside—but inside, you're worn thin. You're tired of carrying the pressure, tired of feeling like no one sees how hard it is.

Elijah's story is your permission slip:

It's OK to rest.

It's OK not to be OK.

It's OK to stop and listen for the whisper.

You don't have to push through burnout.

You don't have to "pray harder" or "fake joy."

You have to be honest—and let God meet you in the stillness.

So, take time to breathe.

Step outside.

Journal.

Cry.

Sit in silence.

Let the noise fall away long enough to hear that whisper: "I'm here. I see you. I'm not leaving."

Even in the chaos, you are not forgotten.

And even when everything feels uncertain, you are being held by a God who speaks gently—and never lets go.

Pause & Reflect

- Have you ever felt like you were at your breaking point—even after something went "right"?

- Where might God be inviting you to rest and hear His whisper?

One last thing to remember:

You don't need louder faith—sometimes, you need a quiet space to breathe.

***

When Life Gets Hard: A Final Word from Chapter 2

Life isn't always smooth.

Sometimes, it feels like one hard thing after another—stress at school, friendship drama, family tension, or the heavy weight of not feeling OK and not knowing why. You try to hold it together, but inside, it's a swirl of doubt, exhaustion, and quiet questions like, "Is it always going to feel *This heavy*?"

If you've felt that way, you're not alone.

Every story in this chapter was about someone who hit a wall. Someone who faced something overwhelming, scary, or soul-crushing—and somehow, with God, made it through.

- Job lost everything—but even in his grief, he clung to his faith.

- Daniel was thrown into a den of lions, but knew he was never alone.

- Jonah ran from his calling—and still, grace found him.

- Nehemiah rebuilt what was broken—stone by stone, through fear and resistance.

- Paul wrote letters of encouragement from prison because his mission mattered more than his pain.

- And Elijah? Even after a massive spiritual victory, he collapsed in exhaustion—and was met not with a lecture but with a whisper.

These people weren't fearless heroes. They were human.

They doubted.

They ran.

They broke down.

They got back up.

And through it all, **God never let them go**. His strength held them. His voice guided them. His grace restored them.

And he'll do the same for you.

You don't need to be fearless to stay faithful.

You don't need to have it all together to keep moving forward.

God isn't asking you to be perfect—He's just asking you to stay close.

- *Every time you choose hope instead of hiding.*

- *Grace instead of guilt.*

- *Presence instead of performance.*

You're laying down bricks of faith that can weather any storm.

Because here's the truth:

Faith doesn't always take the storm away.

But it will anchor you through it.

So take heart.

You're not broken beyond repair.

You're not alone in the dark.

You're part of something bigger than this moment.

And just like the people you've met on these pages, you *have what it takes* to keep going. One step at a time. One breath. One prayer.

The storm may still be swirling.

But your foundation?

It's unshakable.

***

Pause & Reflect

- Which story in this chapter felt most like your own—and why?

- What's one step you can take today to stay anchored in faith, even if the storm doesn't stop?

One last thing to remember:

God isn't asking you to be fearless—He's just asking you to stay close.

Looking Ahead: From Surviving to Thriving — A Journey of Hope and Growth

You've just walked through a chapter filled with storms—pressure, fear, heartbreak, and the overwhelming weight of not having it all together. If you saw yourself in those stories—if you felt the sting of struggle or the ache of waiting—you're not alone.

But here's the truth: faith isn't just about surviving what hurts.

It's about discovering who you're becoming on the other side of it.

Each person you met—Job, Daniel, Jonah, Nehemiah, Paul, Elijah—walked through fire. But they didn't come out the same.

They came out wiser.

More rooted in who they were and who God is.

And now, that's where we're headed next.

This next chapter is about more than just holding on.

It's about growing.

Thriving.

Becoming someone who lives out their faith—not just in the challenging moments, but in the everyday.

So, what does it look like to build something lasting?

How do you grow spiritually when life feels okay?

How do you keep your connection to God strong when the pressure isn't as loud?

We'll discuss real things—how your faith influences your self-worth, how it guides your friendships, and how it impacts your decisions.

Because following Jesus isn't just about reacting to life—it's about walking forward with purpose, peace, and strength.

Faith was never meant to be a lifeline, only for the hard times.

It's a foundation for your entire life.

So take a deep breath. You've already come so far.

Let's keep going—and start building something that lasts.

Chapter 3

Building Meaningful Relationships

F riendship can be complicated.

One day, you're laughing until your sides hurt, and the next, you're staring at a "read" message, wondering why someone suddenly stopped texting back. In a world of group chats, shifting alliances, and "besties" who can disappear overnight, building something real and lasting can feel rare.

But here's the truth:

You were created for connection.

Not just surface-level friends but relationships that *see* you, support you, and help you grow.

This chapter examines the nature of those relationships. Not perfect—but powerful. And it begins with one of the most beautiful and surprising friendships in the Bible: **Jonathan and David.**

***

Jonathan and David: Choosing Loyalty Over Comfort

Their friendship shouldn't have worked.

David was the rising star—the giant slayer everyone was talking about. Jonathan was the crown prince—the one who, by every earthly measure, should've been David's rival. David's success meant Jonathan's future as king was fading.

But instead of letting jealousy grow, Jonathan made a bold choice:

He chose friendship.

From the moment they met, something clicked. The Bible says their souls were "*knit together*" (**1 Samuel 18:1**). This wasn't about shared hobbies or convenience; it was about a profound spiritual connection. It was a deep, spiritual bond rooted in loyalty, trust, and faith.

Jonathan didn't just encourage David—he honored him.

He gave David his robe, armor, sword, bow, and belt. These weren't just hand-me-downs. They were symbols of his authority, power, and future. And by giving them to David, Jonathan was saying:

"*I see who God is calling you to be. And I'm for you—even if it costs me.*"

That kind of friendship is rare.

And it's brave.

Celebrating someone else's calling—especially when it seems to conflict with your own—takes humility. It takes a love that isn't about competition or control but about believing in the God-given potential of someone else and cheering it on.

But their friendship wasn't just tested in the palace—it was tested in the fire.

Jonathan's father, **King Saul**, grew dangerously jealous of David. His anger turned into threats. Then, into action. David's life was at risk. And Jonathan had a choice:

Side with his father.

Or protect his friend.

He chose to protect.

Jonathan warned David. He risked his safety to stand in the gap. And when the moment came for them to say goodbye, Jonathan wept—and blessed David with these words:

"Go in peace. We have sworn friendship with each other in the name of the Lord" (**1 Samuel 20:42**).

Their bond? It outlasted fear.

Outlasted pressure.

Outlasted death.

After Jonathan died in battle, David never forgot him. He kept his promise, even seeking out Jonathan's son years later to show kindness in his name. Their friendship didn't just shape their hearts—it shaped David's leadership, his legacy, and his faith.

What This Means for You

You don't have to be a prince or a warrior to build meaningful friendships.

You have to be willing to love selflessly, speak truthfully, and show up—especially when it's hard.

That means:

- **Standing by your friends** when it would be easier to walk away.

- **Celebrating their success**, even while you're still waiting for yours.

- **Saying "I'm here,"** even when things get awkward or complicated.

In a world full of highlight reels, real friendship is radical.

It's not about followers or filters—it's about who shows up when no one else does.

So ask yourself:

- Who are the Jonathans in your life—those who show up, believe in you, and speak truth over you even when it's uncomfortable?

- And, more importantly, **who are you being a Jonathan to?**

When friendship is rooted in faith, it doesn't just make life easier; it also brings a deeper meaning to life.

It makes you braver.

Wiser.

More fully *you*.

Because the best friendships don't just walk beside you—they help you become who God made you to be.

Pause & Reflect

- Who in your life supports your calling, even when it doesn't benefit them?

- How can you show up for a friend this week with loyalty, honesty, or sacrifice?

One last thing to remember:

True friendship isn't about gaining influence—it's about giving support.

***

Mary and Martha: When Being Present Matters Most

Sometimes, we think love has to look like doing everything—being everywhere, handling it all, and making sure no one's disappointed.

But what if some of the most meaningful relationships in your life don't need more of your effort?

Do they need more of *you*?

That's the heart of Mary and Martha's story, found in **Luke 10:38-42**.

Jesus was coming to visit—not just a teacher or a guest, but their close friend—someone they deeply loved and respected.

You can almost picture the moment:

Martha rushed around the house, checking the bread, adjusting the cushions, and making sure everything was just right. She was doing what many of us do when someone important shows up: trying to make it perfect.

Mary chose a different approach.

She sat.

She paused.

She put aside what could wait and focused on the one thing that mattered most at that moment: **being with Jesus**.

Now, Martha wasn't wrong for working hard. Her effort came from love.

But in all her doing, she missed the deeper invitation—one that Mary quietly accepted.

When Martha finally spoke up in frustration, Jesus didn't dismiss her. He responded with both kindness and truth:

"Martha, Martha, you are worried and upset about many things, but few things are needed—or indeed only one. Mary has chosen what is better, and nobody will take it away from her." (Luke 10:41-42, NIV)

He wasn't scolding her for caring—He was gently redirecting her heart.

Jesus saw her stress. He knew her intentions were good.

But he reminded her that love isn't measured by performance.

It's deepened through **presence**.

Why This Still Matters

We live in a world that glorifies hustle.

Productivity.

Constant motion.

And while there's nothing wrong with being responsible or driven, it's easy to believe that your *worth*—or your *relationships*—depends on how much you do.

But Jesus showed us something different.

Something quieter.

Something stronger.

Sometimes, the most powerful gift you can offer is your full attention.

To be fully present in a conversation, rather than being distracted by your phone.

To listen instead of rushing to solve.

To choose connection over perfection.

Balancing Martha's Heart with Mary's Posture

You might feel more like Martha—always on the move, constantly checking in, always holding things together.

That's not a flaw. It's part of what makes you strong, dependable, and deeply loving.

But don't forget:

You're allowed to sit down, too.

You're allowed to slow down.

To breathe.

To rest in the moment without guilt.

Proper balance isn't about becoming someone else.

It's about learning when it's time to serve and when it's time to be still.

In relationships, **both** matter.

Being Present with the People Who Matter

Whether it's your family, friends, or your relationship with God, presence changes everything.

It's what creates space for authentic connection.

It's what builds trust.

It's what makes people feel truly seen.

You don't need the perfect words or flawless plans to love someone well.

Sometimes, the most healing thing you can offer is your quiet attention.

Your undivided time.

Your willingness to sit with someone in the joy, the mess, or the uncertainty.

Mary's choice wasn't dramatic.

It wasn't flashy.

But it was life-changing.

And you can make that same choice—day by day, moment by moment.

So the next time your calendar is complete, your notifications are buzzing, and everything feels urgent.

Pause.

Ask yourself:

- *What matters most right now?*

- *Am I showing up for the people who matter?*

- *And where is Jesus in this moment?*

You don't have to do more to be loved more.

You are already loved—completely, deeply, freely.

Sometimes, the most sacred act of love is simply being present.

With God.

With others.

And even with yourself.

Pause & Reflect

- Do you tend to be more like Martha or Mary in your relationships?

- What's one small way you can practice presence this week?

One last thing to remember:

Love isn't proven by performance—it's grown through presence.

***

Abraham and Lot: Choosing Peace When Conflict Hits Close to Home

Family can be your most significant support—and sometimes, your biggest challenge.

One moment, you're laughing over dinner. Next, you're stuck in a silent standoff, unsure what just went wrong. When emotions run deep, even minor disagreements can feel like earthquakes.

That's what makes the story of Abraham and Lot so powerful.

You can find it in **Genesis 13**—a short but rich chapter about peace, space, and perspective.

They started their journey together—uncle and nephew, side by side—leaving everything behind to follow God's call into the unknown. As they traveled, both men prospered. Their herds grew. Their wealth increased.

Life was good until it got too crowded.

Soon, the land could no longer support them both. Arguments broke out—not between Abraham and Lot directly, but between their herders. The tension simmered. The atmosphere shifted. And Abraham had a choice:

Pretend everything was fine—or face the conflict with wisdom and love.

He chose peace.

Abraham didn't wait for things to explode. He approached Lot—not with blame or frustration-but with gentleness.

"Let's not have any quarreling between you and me," he said, *"for we are close relatives"* (**Genesis 13:8**).

Then, in a surprising act of humility, he gave Lot his first choice of land:

"If you go left, I'll go right. If you go right, I'll go left."

Abraham didn't have to do that. He was older. He was the leader. By every cultural standard, the choice was his.

But Abraham chose **relationship over rights**.

Peace over pride.

Lot looked out over the land and picked what appeared to be the best: the lush plains near Sodom. It was visually impressive, materially promising, but spiritually risky.

What appeared to be good on the surface came with hidden consequences.

Abraham settled in Canaan. It didn't sparkle like Sodom. But God was there. And after they parted ways, God reaffirmed His promise to Abraham:

"Look around... all the land that you see I will give to you and your offspring forever" (**Genesis 13:14–15**).

What This Means for You

Sometimes, the best way to protect a relationship is to create **space.**

That doesn't mean cutting people off. It means recognizing when peace needs room to breathe.

Abraham didn't slam a door. He opened one for conversation, for mutual respect, for long-term healing. His choice reminds us that conflict doesn't have to destroy connection.

You might not be dividing the land with your cousin.

But maybe you've felt the tension with someone you care about—a sibling who pushes your buttons, a parent who doesn't get it, a friend who keeps crossing a line.

Abraham shows us that **love can lead**, even when letting go is part of the process.

Handling Conflict Without Losing Connection

Abraham wasn't passive. He was wise.

He didn't avoid the issue. He named it, addressed it, and offered a peaceful solution that honored both sides.

That's the kind of maturity God invites us to grow into.

You don't have to fix everything with a dramatic gesture.

Start small:

- **Listen to understand**, not just to defend.

- **Speak calmly**, even when you feel hurt.

- **Take a breath** before reacting.

- **Walk away if needed**, not to punish, but to protect peace.

Choosing peace doesn't make you weak; it makes you strong.

It makes you strong enough to value people more than your point.

Looking Beneath the Surface

Lot's choice seemed bright in the moment.

But being near Sodom exposed him and his family to compromise and danger.

It's a quiet warning:

Sometimes, the path that looks easiest now comes with regret later.

Abraham's choice looked less glamorous, but it came with God's continued **presence, favor, and promise**.

There's wisdom in slowing down, in seeking peace, and in trusting God to bless the road that honors Him.

The Bigger Picture

Conflict is a regular part of every close relationship.

What shapes your character isn't whether it happens, but *how you handle it.*

You won't always be able to solve every problem.

But you can:

- *Show grace.*

- *Stay kind.*

- *Be the one who values peace over pride.*

Abraham modeled a kind of strength that didn't need to win, because he already knew where his blessing came from.

Ultimately, **peace isn't the absence of conflict**.

It's the *presence of God* in the middle of it.

Pause & Reflect

- Is there someone in your life you need to make peace with, or give space to?

- What would it look like to value the relationship more than being "right"?

One last thing to remember:

You don't have to win the argument to protect the relationship. Sometimes, peace is the greatest strength.

***

The Prodigal Son: When Forgiveness Feels Impossible—But Isn't

Sometimes, the people closest to us hurt us the most.

And sometimes, *we're* the ones who mess up.

That's what makes the story of the **Prodigal Son**, found in **Luke 15:11-32**, so powerful.

It's not just about a reckless kid making bad choices.

It's about what happens when love is tested, trust is broken, and someone dares to come home anyway.

The Bold Ask

It all starts with a shocking request.

The younger son turns to his father and says, *"Give me my share of the inheritance now."*

Not later. Not when the time is right. **Now.**

In that culture, this was like saying, *"I'm done with this family. I want out."*

It was bold. Disrespectful. Heartbreaking.

But the father agrees—and watches his son walk away.

What follows is predictable: partying, reckless spending, and chasing every thrill. But soon, the money runs out. The friends disappear. The highs fade.

Reality hits hard.

The son ends up broke, hungry, and alone, reduced to feeding pigs and wishing he could eat their food. It's the lowest of lows.

And then something shifts.

He starts to remember.

Not just the food or the comfort he left behind, but the *love*.

He remembers the father who raised him. The home he walked away from—the life he once had.

And for the first time in a long time, he sees clearly—not just the mess he's made, but the *heart that might still be waiting.*

So he begins the journey back.

Not as a son, he thinks—but maybe as a servant. *Maybe*, just maybe, he can earn a place on the edge of home.

The Moment Everything Changes

Here's the twist.

The father doesn't wait for the knock on the door.

He runs—**runs**—to meet his son.

Before the son can even finish his apology, the father embraces him. No shaming. No cold shoulder. No, "I told you so."

Just open arms. And a heart that never stopped hoping.

He calls for a robe. A ring. A feast.

Not as a reward, but as a celebration.

"This son of mine was dead and is alive again; he was lost and is found." **(Luke 15:24)**

This is forgiveness without conditions.

Love without limits.

It's a glimpse of how **God sees us** when we wander, mess up, and wonder if we've gone too far.

But Then There's the Older Brother

Not everyone is celebrating.

The older brother—faithful, responsible, steady—hears the music and gets angry.

"How is this fair?" he asks.

"I've been here the whole time, doing everything right. And he gets a party?"

Can you blame him?

His reaction is raw. Honest. Real.

That feeling of being overlooked while someone else gets grace? It stings.

But the father meets him, too.

"Everything I have is yours," he says.

"But we had to celebrate—your brother was lost, and now he's found."

We don't know how the older brother responds.

The story ends without resolution. And that's the point.

Because **grace is uncomfortable**.

It messes with our sense of fairness.

It reaches past what's earned and offers what's *needed*—healing, wholeness, and welcome.

What This Means for You

Perhaps you identify with the younger son—the one who made mistakes, drifted, and wondered if it was too late to come home.

Or maybe you feel more like the older brother—loyal but overlooked, questioning someone else's second chance.

Either way, this story is for you.

It reminds us that **no failure is final**.

That we're never too far gone.

That *coming home is always an option*—even when we feel unworthy.

It also invites us to examine our hearts when others are shown grace.

Because sometimes the most challenging part of forgiveness isn't receiving it

It's *extending* it.

When Forgiveness Feels Too Hard

Let's be honest—real-life reconciliation doesn't always look like a hug and a feast.

Sometimes, it takes time.

Hard conversations.

Boundaries.

Healing.

Forgiveness isn't about pretending the hurt didn't happen; it's about acknowledging it and moving forward.

It's about choosing not to let that hurt *define* you anymore.

It starts small:

- A *willingness to soften.*
- A *decision to stop replaying the pain.*
- A *prayer for the courage to let go.*

Forgiveness may not erase the past, but it *can* change the future.

It can rebuild what was broken.

It can open the door to something new.

Whether You're Trying to Forgive or Be Forgiven

Remember this:

You are **not** at your worst moment.

You are more than your mistakes.

And the door—whatever "home" looks like for you—is still open.

Pause & Reflect

- Do you see yourself more in the younger son or the older brother right now?

- What would it look like to take one step toward forgiveness—either giving it or receiving it?

One last thing to remember:

Grace doesn't always feel fair, but it always leads us home.

✳✳✳

Naomi and Ruth: When Loyalty Becomes a Lifeline

Some friendships are built slowly—through shared memories, inside jokes, and everyday laughter.

Others are forged in fire.

In grief.

In the ashes of loss—and the choice to stay anyway.

That's where we meet Naomi and Ruth.

You can find their story in the **Book of Ruth, chapters 1–4**—a short yet compelling glimpse of how faith and loyalty can transform emptiness into a legacy.

Naomi had lost everything—her husband, her two sons, and the future she had once imagined. Her world had collapsed in a foreign land. All that remained were her two daughters-in-law, Orpah and Ruth.

With nothing left to offer, Naomi urged them to return to their families.

"Go back," she said.

"Start fresh. Don't waste your lives on my brokenness."

Orpah kissed her goodbye.

But Ruth stayed.

And her words still echo with fierce devotion:

"Where you go, I will go. Where you stay, I will stay. Your people will be my people, and your God, my God."(**Ruth 1:16**)

This wasn't just loyalty.

It was love—brave, selfless, grounded-in-faith love.

Ruth wasn't clinging to the past. She was choosing a future—one where Naomi wouldn't have to walk alone.

And together, they returned to Bethlehem—two widows with empty hands but hearts tethered in trust.

On that quiet road, something beautiful began:

The slow rebuilding of hope.

Loyalty That Leans In

Ruth didn't just speak devotion—she lived it.

Once they arrived in Bethlehem, Ruth went straight to work. Day after day, she gathered leftover grain in the fields to keep them fed. It wasn't glamorous. It wasn't easy. But it was love in motion.

Then came Boaz.

A man of honor and kindness, Boaz noticed Ruth, not just her beauty but also her **character**. He saw the quiet strength in how she cared for Naomi. He protected her. He provided for her.

Eventually, he offered something more: his hand in marriage.

This wasn't a fairy tale. It was redemption.

Two lives—once marked by loss—are now being restored in ways they couldn't have planned.

Together, Ruth and Boaz had a son named **Obed**.

That child would become the grandfather of **King David** and part of the family line that would lead to **Jesus** Himself.

All because of a woman who *refused to walk away*.

Faith That Holds You Together

What bound Naomi and Ruth wasn't just shared pain.

It was **faith**.

Ruth wasn't raised in Naomi's faith. She came from a different culture and a different belief system. But she made a bold, quiet decision—not just to follow Naomi, but to follow her *God*.

Her faith wasn't inherited.

It was *chosen*.

And that shared faith became their anchor.

Through grief, uncertainty, and the hard work of starting over, they leaned into God—and into each other. They weren't just surviving. They were rebuilding.

Their story reminds us that faith doesn't just connect us to God; it also connects us.

It lays the foundation for friendships that last, that heal, and that help carry us through seasons we never saw coming.

What Ruth and Naomi Teach Us About Real Friendship

Real friendship isn't always loud.

Sometimes, it's just quietly showing up when someone needs you most.

It's choosing to stay when it would be easier to leave.

It's speaking hope when everything feels heavy.

If you want that kind of connection in your life, start here:

- **Show up**—especially when it's inconvenient.

- **Ask how someone's doing**—and listen without rushing.

- **Celebrate their wins** as if they were your own.

- **Stick around**—even when things get complicated.

Friendship rooted in loyalty isn't about having perfect answers; it's about being loyal.

It's about being *present*.

And presence, especially in hard times, speaks volumes.

You Don't Have to Do Life Alone

Ruth didn't rescue Naomi.

But she didn't let her walk alone, either.

Maybe you're not facing a loss like theirs.

But you *may* know what it's like to feel empty.

To struggle silently.

Or to wonder how to support someone who's falling apart.

Sometimes, the most powerful thing you can say is:

"I'm not leaving."

Whether you're the one holding on or the one being held—remember:

There is strength in loyalty.

There is beauty in staying close.

There is *hope* in walking together, even when everything feels broken.

Because when friendship is wrapped in faith, it becomes more than support.

It becomes *sacred.*

Pause & Reflect

- Who has stuck by you in hard seasons, and how did their presence shape your story?

- Is there someone in your life who needs to hear, "I'm with you, no matter what"?

One last thing to remember:

You don't have to fix everything to be a faithful friend—sometimes just staying is enough.

***

Peter and Jesus: Trust Through Trials

Some relationships shape us not because they're perfect, but because they survive the most challenging moments.

That's the story of **Peter and Jesus**, found throughout the Gospels, especially in **Luke 22**, **John 21**, and the book of **Acts**.

When Jesus first called Peter, it was simple:

"Follow me."

And Peter did. He dropped his net, walked away from everything he knew, and stepped into something new. No plan. No map. Just trust.

That moment of trust became the foundation of something powerful, messy at times, but transformational.

Peter was bold. Passionate. Quick to speak and quick to act.

He walked on water—but sank when fear hit.

He promised loyalty, but denied Jesus three times when the pressure got real.

He meant well. But he was human.

And when it counted most, he broke.

When You Mess Up Big—But Grace Meets You There

Peter's denial wasn't subtle.

As Jesus was arrested, Peter stood nearby, watching, anxious, afraid.

Three times, someone asked if he knew Jesus.

Three times, he said no.

"I don't know Him."

And when the rooster crowed—just as Jesus had predicted—Peter broke down.

He had failed. Deeply. Publicly. And he knew it.

But failure didn't get the final word.

After His resurrection, Jesus came to Peter, not with condemnation, but with restoration.

He asked Peter:

"Do you love me?"

Three times. One for each denial.

And after each answer, Jesus responded:

"Feed my sheep."

He wasn't punishing Peter.

He was *rebuilding* him.

Calling him *back* to the purpose.

Lifting him *into* the future.

From Brokenness to Boldness

The Peter we see after the resurrection?

Still bold. Still passionate.

But now, *refined by grace.*

He stood up at Pentecost and preached with fire. He led the early church. He mentored believers and spread the gospel that had changed him forever.

Peter went from *denying Jesus* to *avowing Him.*

Not because he became stronger on his own, but because he allowed grace to reshape him.

How This Translates to You

Maybe you've let someone down.

Maybe someone's let *you* down.

Perhaps you're afraid that one moment will ruin everything. Or maybe you're scared to trust again.

Peter's story reminds us:

- **Trust takes time.** Jesus walked with Peter through every high and low.

- **Failure isn't final.** Your worst moment doesn't define your worth.

- **Grace restores.** God doesn't just forgive—He *rebuilds*.

Want Stronger Friendships? Start Here.

Relationships like Peter and Jesus' are built on trust, and trust grows through consistency, honesty, and grace.

- **Be honest about your flaws**. Vulnerability builds connection.

- **Stick around after the mess-ups.** Loyalty matters more than perfection.

- **Encourage growth.** Speak life into your people.

- **Forgive.** It frees both your heart and theirs.

You don't need flawless friends.

You need *faithful* ones.

And you can be one, too.

Looking Back to Move Forward

This chapter wasn't just about relationships—it was about becoming.

You saw selfless friendship in **Jonathan and David**.

Presence over pressure in **Mary and Martha**.

The power of peace in **Abraham and Lot**.

Radical forgiveness in **the Prodigal Son**.

Unshakable loyalty in **Naomi and Ruth**.

And healing grace in **Peter and Jesus**.

These relationships weren't perfect.

But they were real.

Through them, we saw how love, trust, and faith can transform even the most broken connection into something beautiful.

When Relationships Shape Who You're Becoming

Relationships shape us—sometimes slowly, sometimes all at once.

They have the power to lift you or tear you down.

But when they're rooted in **grace**, **honesty**, and **faith**, they can help you grow into the person you were made to be.

So ask yourself:

Who has stood by me in the hard seasons?

Who do I need to forgive—or be honest with?

Where can I show up more fully, more gently, more graciously?

Who is helping me become the person God created me to be?

You're not expected to have it all figured out.

But as you learn to show up for others—and let them show up for you—something shifts.

You become someone who listens more deeply.

Loves more freely.

Forgives more quickly.

And stands more firmly.

You become someone who reflects God's love through every relationship.

Pause & Reflect

- Which story in this chapter challenged or encouraged you most?

- What's one way you can strengthen a relationship in your life this week—through honesty, presence, grace, or boundaries?

One last thing to remember:

Great relationships aren't perfect. But with love and trust, they can be life-changing.

Looking Ahead: Choices That Shape You

Faith isn't just about believing the right things—it's about choosing how you live, even when no one's watching.

Maybe you've been in those moments where you're unsure which way to go. A decision feels heavy. The pressure to impress or fit in is real. Or you've caught yourself wondering, *"Does this even matter?"*

Here's the truth:

Every choice—big or small—shapes the kind of person you're becoming.

And when your decisions are rooted in wisdom, courage, and truth, they don't just shape your future—they reflect your faith.

In this next chapter, you'll meet people who stood at a crossroads:

- Some chose integrity.

- Some gave in to fear or pride.

- All of them demonstrate how powerful our choices truly are.

Remember, you don't have to be perfect. We all make mistakes, and that's okay. What's important is that you're willing to learn and grow from them.

What you need is the willingness to pause, listen, and choose with intention. This is where your power lies, in the conscious decisions you make every day.

Let's explore how faith can guide your decisions and how even the smallest acts of trust can lead to a life of strength, purpose, and impact. Remember, it's not the size of the act that matters but the intention and faith behind it.

REVIEW US!

What did you think?
If something in this book stuck with you, take a sec
to leave a quick review—it helps others find it too.

Scan below to share your thoughts.

Making Wise Choices

P icture this: you're standing at a crossroads.

One path looks easy. Another looks exciting. A third seems safe. But deep down, you know only one of them truly aligns with **who you're becoming**—the version of you God is shaping every day.

Making choices is a constant part of life, especially in your teen years.

From friendships to school to how you spend your time, every decision—big or small—adds a brick to the foundation of your future.

And while impulse can shout, **wisdom whispers**.

It helps you pause.

Look ahead.

And ask, *"Who do I want to be on the other side of this decision?"*

That's what wisdom is all about.

It's not just knowing right from wrong.

It's **understanding what matters most**.

It's choosing the path that leads to growth, even when it's harder in the moment.

It's trusting God's voice more than the noise around you.

It's learning to listen—not just to what feels good now, but to what will still feel right later.

Wisdom sees beyond the now.

It invites you to live with intention rather than react.

In this chapter, we'll walk through stories of people—young and old—who faced life-defining choices:

Some listened to God's leading. Others ignored it. And in each case, we'll see what wisdom looks like when it's lived out and what happens when it's not.

Because your choices don't just shape your circumstances.

They shape your *character*.

And when you build your life with wisdom, you're not just surviving—you're becoming someone strong, steady, and ready for whatever comes next.

Solomon's Story: Asking for What Matters Most

(*Read it in 1 Kings 3*)

When Solomon became king, he was young and inexperienced.

He didn't pretend to have it all figured out.

He didn't fake strength.

He prayed.

But what he asked for might surprise you.

He didn't ask for riches.

He didn't ask for revenge.

He didn't even ask for success.

He asked God for **wisdom**.

Think about that.

Of all the things he could've chosen—power, popularity, security—Solomon chose understanding. He asked for a heart that could discern between right and wrong. And God honored that request.

Solomon's wisdom became legendary. It shaped how he led. It influenced how he solved problems. And it blessed everyone around him.

The Moment That Defined His Wisdom

One of Solomon's most well-known moments came when two women came before him, both claiming to be the mother of the same baby.

There were no DNA tests. No cameras. There is no clear evidence. It's just a deeply emotional, high-stakes situation.

Solomon didn't panic.

He didn't guess.

He proposed something shocking:

"Cut the baby in half and give each woman a part."

Immediately, one of the women cried out, *"No—let her have the child!"*

And in that instant, Solomon knew **she** was the birth mother. She loved the child too much to see him harmed.

That one moment revealed more than cleverness.

It showed **discernment. Compassion. Courage.**

Wisdom doesn't just solve problems—it *sees people.*

It protects what's sacred.

Wisdom That Shapes a Life—and a Nation

Solomon's wisdom didn't stay in the throne room.

It shaped how he built the **temple**.

How he managed **alliances**.

He led **with peace** in a time that had long been marked by war.

People traveled from faraway lands to hear him speak. His reputation stretched across kingdoms.

But the more profound truth?

It all started with **one decision**.

He didn't ask for a crown that sparkled.

He asked for a heart that listened.

And that choice?

It changed everything.

How Wisdom Applies to You—Right Now

You might not be ruling a kingdom, but you're ruling *your own life.*

Every day, you're making choices:
What to believe. Who to trust. How to treat people. Where to go next.

And sometimes, the right decision isn't obvious.

That's okay.

Wisdom isn't about being perfect.

It's about being *teachable*. Curious. Willing to ask questions and seek the truth before charging ahead.

It's about pausing when pressure tells you to rush.

It's about remembering who you want to become on the other side of the decision.

And here's the good news:

Wisdom isn't reserved for kings.

It's available to *you*.

James 1:5 says: *"If any of you lacks wisdom, you should ask God, who gives generously to all without finding fault, and it will be given to you."*

So ask.

Before you post. Before you react. Before you go along just because "everyone else is doing it."

Ask:

- *Is this wise?*

- *Will this bring peace or regret?*

- *Is this helping me grow, or pulling me away from who I'm becoming?*

The wisest people in your life may not be the ones with the loudest voices.

They're the ones who live in *peace*.

Who makes others feel safe.

Who knows when to speak—and when to listen?

What We Learn From Solomon

Solomon's story reminds us:

- **Wise decisions are often quiet ones.** They're made in stillness, not in chaos.

- **Wisdom begins with humility.** It starts when we acknowledge that we don't know everything.

- **Seeking God's perspective brings peace** not only to your life but also to those around you.

So the next time you're standing at a crossroads, unsure of what to do, remember Solomon.

Remember the king who could've asked for anything, but chose wisdom instead.

And know:

That same wisdom is also available to you.

Pause & Reflect

- What's one decision you're facing right now that could use more wisdom and less pressure?

- Have you taken the time to ask God for guidance, or are you trying to figure it out on your own?

One last thing to remember:

Wisdom doesn't always shout—but it always leads somewhere better.

***

Gideon's Army: Trusting God's Plan Over Popular Opinion

(*Read it in Judges 6–7*)

Imagine this: You're chosen to lead a primary mission, but you don't feel remotely qualified.

You're not the strongest, the loudest, or the most confident—and yet, the assignment lands in your lap.

That was Gideon's reality.

When God called him to lead Israel's army against the powerful Midianites, Gideon's initial response wasn't one of bold confidence.

There was *doubt*.

He asked for proof.

Twice.

He laid out a fleece, asking for dew to fall only on the fleece, not on the ground. Then, just to be sure, he reversed the request.

Sound familiar?

Maybe you haven't used fleeces—but perhaps you've whispered late-night prayers like:

"God, if this is really You, give me a sign."

Gideon's story doesn't begin with bravado.

It begins with honest questions.

And God didn't shame him for that.

He *met him in it* with patience, confirmation, and a quiet invitation to trust.

When God's Math Doesn't Make Sense

Once Gideon was all in, he assembled an army of 32,000 men. Not bad, but still way smaller than the Midianite force.

Then God said:

"Too many."

Wait—**what?**

God told Gideon to let anyone afraid go home. That left 10,000.

There are still too many.

Next came a strange test at the water's edge.

Only 300 men were chosen.

From 32,000 to 300.

The odds weren't just bad—they were *laughable*.

But that was the point.

God wasn't looking for a win that could be credited to strength or strategy.

He wanted Israel to know:

This victory is Mine.

And I'll do it my way.

Gideon obeyed—even when the plan looked completely upside down.

No swords. No sneak attacks. Just torches, clay jars, and trumpets.

Victory by Faith, Not Force

In the middle of the night, Gideon and his 300 men surrounded the Midianite camp.

At his signal, they **smashed their jars**, **raised their torches**, and **blasted their trumpets**.

The noise. The light. The surprise.

The Midianites panicked, turned on each other, and fled in terror.

Victory.

Without a single sword drawn by Gideon's men.

This wasn't just a military win.

It was a **faith moment**.

Proof that God doesn't need perfect odds to show up powerfully.

He often chooses the unlikely path, so that we'll know it was *Him* all along.

Gideon's courage didn't come from flawless planning or overwhelming numbers.

It came from trusting the One who called him, even when the math didn't make sense.

Faith Over Fear, Trust Over Control

We're taught to believe bigger is better.

More followers. More backup. More guarantees.

But Gideon's story flips that upside down.
Faith doesn't always look logical.

It doesn't always feel safe.

And it rarely follows the crowd.

You might not be on a battlefield, but you'll face choices that feel just as intimidating:

Do I speak up or stay silent?

Do I follow what's right, or what's popular?

Do I trust God's voice, or play it safe?

In those moments, **remember Gideon**.

You don't need to have all the answers, all the resources, or all the confidence.

You need a heart that's willing to say: "God, *if this is You—I'm in.*"

What We Learn From Gideon

Gideon's journey reminds us that:

- **God uses ordinary people** for extraordinary things.

- **Faith often starts with fear, but it doesn't end there**.

- **Obedience matters more than optics.**

- **God's plans may not always make sense, but they're always good.**

So, if you feel small, unsure, or like you're not ready, you're in good company.

Gideon wasn't ready either.

But he said yes anyway.

And God used him to accomplish something only *He* could have pulled off.

Pause & Reflect

- Have you ever felt like Gideon—unsure if you're the "right" person for something God might be calling you to do?

- Is there an area of your life where you need to trade control for trust?

One last thing to remember:

When you follow God's lead, even small steps can lead to massive victories.

The Rich Young Ruler: The Cost of Materialism

(Read it in Mark 10:17–27)

Imagine a young man who appears to have everything—wealth, influence, a spotless reputation, and a promising future. He's not arrogant or fake. He's *sincere*. He runs up to Jesus, kneels with respect, and asks a question that lives quietly in many of our hearts:

"What must I do to inherit eternal life?"

He wasn't trying to trap Jesus. He wasn't showing off.

He was searching for something real. Something lasting.

Because deep down, despite his full bank account, *he felt empty*.

Jesus looked at him with love.

He began with what the man already knew:

"You know the commandments..."

And the young man smiled.

"I've kept all those since I was a boy," he replied.

But Jesus wasn't done.

He looked past the resume, past the performance, and into the place where fear still lived. Then He said something bold, something beautiful—and something heartbreaking:

"One thing you lack. Sell everything you have, give to the poor, and you will have treasure in heaven. Then come, follow me."

The young man's face fell.

His shoulders dropped.

And he walked away, *grieving*.

Why?

Because his possessions didn't just take up space in his home.

They had taken up space in his **heart**.

When Good Things Become Ultimate Things

Jesus wasn't telling everyone to drain their savings.

He was revealing what was **competing with God** for first place.

This man had built his identity on being a good person.

On being successful.

On being in control.

He wanted to follow Jesus—but not if it meant letting go of what made him feel safe, important, and secure.

And Jesus didn't chase him.

He didn't soften the truth or negotiate a compromise.

Instead, He turned to His disciples and said:

"How hard it is for the rich to enter the kingdom of God."

Not because money is evil.

But because wealth, comfort, and image can **numb us** to our need for grace.

They blur the lines between what we *own* and *who we are*.

What We Hold Onto Can Hold Us Back

Most of us won't face a single, dramatic choice to give up everything we own.

But we face *smaller versions* of that decision all the time.

- The choice to be generous when we'd rather keep.

- The choice to speak honestly when we'd rather stay silent.

- The choice to say no to something shiny so we can say yes to something *holy.*

The rich young ruler didn't walk away because he didn't care.

He walked away because he wasn't *ready to let go.*

It's easy to say, "*I'll follow Jesus.*"

But what happens when He touches something we're clinging to?

What Story Do You Want Your Life to Tell?

Our culture is loud about what matters:

- *Have more.*

- *Be seen more.*

- *Post more.*

- *Hustle harder.*

- *Stay comfortable.*

But deep down, we know:

An oversized closet doesn't mean a whole heart.

And a curated life isn't the same as a meaningful one.

Some of the most joyful people don't have a lot of "stuff"—but they're rich in peace, purpose, and connection.

That's what Jesus wanted for this young man.

Not less joy—**more**.

Not less security—**a deeper one**.

Not just a rule to follow, but a *life of freedom* to step into.

Choosing Simplicity, Generosity, and Purpose

Letting go doesn't mean losing everything; it means gaining something more valuable.

It means holding things **loosely** so God can lead you freely.

Try this:

- Look around your room. Pick one item you value.

Ask yourself: *"If I didn't have this, would I still know who I am?"*

- Make a list of 10 things you're grateful for that money can't buy—like laughter with a friend, a moment of peace, or a deep talk that made you feel seen.

- Practice generosity this week by buying a snack for someone, giving away something you've outgrown, or writing a note of encouragement to someone.

These aren't just "nice" things.

They're *soul-shaping practices.*

They teach your heart to hold less—and love more.

The Invitation Still Stands

Jesus' invitation didn't disappear when the rich young ruler walked away.

It was still there—waiting. Open. Unchanging.

Just like it is for *you.*

Jesus isn't asking you to let go for the sake of sacrifice.

He's asking you to trust that **what He offers is better**.

A life not defined by *what you own,* but by *who you're becoming.*

A heart not cluttered with comparison, but anchored in truth.

Pause & Reflect

- Is there something in your life you might be holding too tightly—something that's slowly taking up space meant for God?

- What would it look like to loosen your grip and live more open-handedly this week?

One last thing to remember:

Jesus didn't call the rich young ruler out to shame him. He called him forward to set him free. He's doing the same for you.

***

Pilate's Decision: Standing Firm Amidst Peer Pressure

(Read it in Matthew 27:11–26)

Picture a man caught between power and principle.

Pontius Pilate, the Roman governor of Judea, stood at a crossroads. In his hands was the fate of Jesus, a man he *knew* was innocent. A man who had stirred no rebellion and broken no Roman laws. Pilate wasn't close with the religious leaders who brought Jesus to him. He saw through their envy and manipulation.

But outside his palace, the crowd grew louder.

Fueled by pressure and politics.

Demanding one outcome: **crucifixion.**

Pilate tried.

He questioned Jesus privately.

He offered to release Him through the Passover tradition.

He even sent Him to Herod, hoping to pass the decision to someone else.

But every effort was drowned out by the mob's relentless cry:

"Crucify Him!"

Caught in a storm of voices, Pilate wavered.

He had the power to choose justice, but **fear crept in**.

Fear of revolt.

Fear of Caesar's wrath.

Fear of what standing alone might cost him.

So he caved.

He washed his hands in front of the crowd—a symbolic move to clear his conscience.

"*I am innocent of this man's blood,*" he said.

But deep down, he knew:

Silence is still a choice.

Choosing *not* to act with integrity is still a significant decision.

The Cost of Silence

Pilate's story is one of hesitation.

Of knowing what's right, but not following through.

He wasn't violent. He didn't shout.

He didn't hammer the nails.

But he allowed injustice to unfold—and *stepped back*.

We all face moments like that.

When we know the right thing, but doing it means standing out.

Risking judgment.

Maybe even losing something.

And in those moments, like Pilate, we're tempted to wash our hands and walk away.

But **courage doesn't come from comfort**.

It comes from conviction.

Why This Story Still Matters

Pilate's choice shaped history—but not in the way he hoped.

His name isn't remembered for wisdom or leadership.

It's remembered for the moment he backed down.

Not because he didn't know better, but because he *did* and didn't act.

It serves as a warning for all of us.

Peer pressure doesn't always shout.

Sometimes, it whispers:

"Just go along with it."

"Don't make it awkward."

"Everyone else is fine with it."

But you weren't made to blend in.

You were made to **stand firm**.

Standing Strong Today

Integrity takes practice.

You can prepare by imagining real-life situations:

- What would you do if a friend pressured you to do something you know is wrong?

- What would you say if your group started excluding someone?

- Would you have the courage to speak—even if no one else did?

You don't need to be the loudest in the room.

However, you *must* be the one who listens to what is right, even when it's quiet.

Pause & Reflect

- Have you ever been in a moment where peer pressure tempted you to go against your values?

- What would it look like to speak up or stand firm next time, even in a small way?

One last thing to remember:

Pilate washed his hands. But doing nothing is still doing something.

Choose courage—even when it costs.

***

Deborah's Leadership: Courage in the Face of Uncertainty

(Read it in Judges 4–5)

Now, imagine a nation in crisis.

Israel was under brutal oppression—overwhelmed by fear, stuck in a cycle of hopelessness.

And now picture the person God raises:

Not a warrior in armor.

Not a king with status.

But a woman sitting beneath a palm tree, offering **wisdom and justice**.

Her name was **Deborah**.

She was a **prophet**. A **judge**. A **leader** in a time when women weren't expected to lead.

But Deborah didn't lead by shouting.

She led by **listening**.

To God.

To people.

To the truth.

When God gave her a mission—to rally Israel's army and confront the powerful general **Sisera**—Deborah didn't flinch.

She called **Barak** to lead the charge.

Barak hesitated.

He said he wouldn't go unless Deborah came with him.

And she said **yes.**

Not to take over.

Not to prove anything.

But to walk alongside him until he found his courage.

Unexpected Heroes, Unshakable Faith

Their army? Just 10,000 men.

Sisera's army? 900 iron chariots and total intimidation.

But God intervened.

A sudden storm turned the battlefield into a muddy mess. The mighty chariots were stuck.

Confusion spread.

And Israel pressed forward—*bold and believing*.

Then came **Jael**—another unexpected woman who took down Sisera in a moment of fearless action.

The victory came not through power but through **faithful obedience**.

Deborah celebrated with a song.

Not about herself.

But about the bravery of those who *showed up*.

Leadership That Inspires—Even Now

Deborah wasn't about position—she was about purpose.

She **ignited courage** in others.

She helped people rise to who God called them to be.

Her story speaks *especially loudly* when you feel small or unsure of your place.

Because Deborah reminds us:

Leadership isn't about being the loudest.

It's about being *faithful in the quiet, brave in the uncertain,* and *present when it matters most*.

Leading With Courage—Right Where You Are

You don't need to wait to be older, have a title, or know everything.

You can lead today by:

- Speaking up when something isn't right.

- Helping others feel seen.

- Staying calm when things get hard.

- Encouraging people to step into *their* calling.

Authentic leadership isn't about the spotlight—it's *about service.*

It's choosing faith over fear.

And like Deborah, when you lead with heart, you help others believe they can, too.

Pause & Reflect

- Where in your life is God asking you to lead by example, by courage, or by encouragement?

- Is there someone around you who needs your support to find *their* bravery?

One last thing to remember:

Deborah didn't want to be noticed. She led so others could rise.

And you can do the same.

***

Ananias and Sapphira: The Danger of Deception

(*Read it in Acts 5:1–11*)

In the early days of the church, something beautiful was happening.

People were living in a deep community—sharing not only their faith but their homes, meals, prayers, and even their possessions. No one was forced to give anything, yet many did **willingly**, selling land and giving the money to support others in need.

It was a radical act of generosity built on **trust**.

But not everyone was sincere.

Ananias and Sapphira sold a piece of land, just like others had.

However, instead of offering the full amount, they **retained part of it**, while pretending to give it all. On the outside, it looked generous.

But underneath?

It was a lie—**carefully planned, agreed upon, and carried out together**.

When Peter confronted Ananias, he didn't ask about money.

The issue wasn't about numbers. It was about the heart.

"You haven't lied to people," Peter said. *"You've lied to God."*

And then—Ananias collapsed.

Right there. Gone.

Later, Sapphira came in, unaware of what had happened.

She repeated the lie.

And the same thing happened to her.

The shock wasn't just physical—it was *spiritual*. The entire community felt the weight of what had just happened. A wave of **reverence** and **sobering awareness** swept through the church.

Why Integrity Matters So Much

This story might feel extreme.

Why such a dramatic consequence?

Because the church was still young, just forming, and in those fragile early days, trust was everything.

If honesty didn't matter, the whole thing could unravel.

This wasn't just about two people lying.

It was about the message their lie sent:

"You can fake faith, and no one will know."

But God does know.

And His Spirit is holy.

He isn't looking for perfection—He's looking for **honesty**.

Integrity wasn't just a personal virtue; it was a fundamental principle. It was the **glue** holding this growing faith family together.

The Real Cost of a Lie

Let's be real—most of us have told a lie.

To avoid a consequence.

To save face.

To make ourselves look better.

To get out of trouble.

But lies rarely stay small.

They grow. They spread. They create distance between people and inside our hearts.

Ananias and Sapphira weren't punished for being stingy.

They were called out for **pretending**.

This isn't a story of "don't mess up"—it's a story of how **destructive hiding can be**.

Because even if people believe the lie, you still know the truth.

And that knowing? It weighs you down.

Choosing Honesty Every Day

Living with integrity doesn't mean you'll never make a mistake.

It means you don't pretend you didn't.

It's about choosing to be **real**, not perfect.

It's about owning your mistakes, telling the truth, and building a life that's strong enough to stand, even when things get hard.

Want to grow in honesty? Start small:

- Pause before you speak. Ask yourself: *Is this true?*

- Be brave enough to admit when you're wrong.

- Surround yourself with friends who call you *up*, not just cheer you on.

- And when you're tempted to lie, ask why. *What are you afraid of?*

The more you practice truth-telling, the **lighter** you'll feel.

Integrity builds more than trust with others.

It builds **peace** within yourself.

Pause & Reflect

- Is there any area of your life where you've been pretending instead of being real?

- What would it feel like to live with nothing to hide?

One last thing to remember:

God doesn't expect you to be perfect. But he does invite you, to be honest.

★★★

Chapter 4 Wrap-Up: Decisions That Define You

Every story in this chapter showed us something powerful:

Solomon asked for wisdom and went on to shape a kingdom.

Gideon trusted a plan that didn't make sense and saw victory.

The **rich young ruler** chose comfort over calling and walked away.

Pilate gave in to pressure and lived with regret.

Deborah led with courage and called others into boldness.

Ananias and Sapphira pretended to be honest and broke the trust that held their community together.

None of these people were perfect.

Some made incredible choices.

Some made painful ones.

But in every case, **their choices shaped who they were becoming**.

And so do yours.

You don't need all the answers to make wise decisions.

You need:

- The **humility** to ask for help.
- The **courage** to act with integrity.
- The **faith** to trust that even small choices matter.

So next time you're standing at a crossroads—big or small—pause.

Breathe.

Ask yourself:

"What kind of person do I want to become?"

Because the truth is...You're already becoming that person—**right now.**

One choice at a time.

Looking Ahead: Faith in Action

So far, in our journey of personal growth and faith in action, you've explored how decisions—both big and small—can shape your character and future. You've seen people choose wisdom, wrestle with fear, resist pressure, and step into leadership, even when it wasn't easy.

Now, it's time to elevate your understanding of faith, to see it not just as a belief but as a transformative force that can shape your actions and the world around you.

In the next chapter, we shift the focus outward to explore how your beliefs can be practically applied to impact the world around you.

We'll examine real-life stories of individuals who stood up for others, challenged injustice, gave sacrificially, and broke through stereotypes. Not because it was popular, but because it was right.

You'll explore what it means to love boldly, act with courage, and live out your values in a world that often looks the other way.

Because faith isn't just about what you believe.

It's about how you live.

As we turn the page, remember that your everyday actions—your compassion, courage, and voice—are not just incidental but integral to the narrative of faith in action. They can and do make a real difference.

The world needs more people who live by their convictions.

And that might start with you.

Chapter 5

Exploring Social Justice and Ethics

Samaritan: A Story of Compassion

(Read it in Luke 10:25–37)

Imagine walking down a busy street and seeing someone collapsed on the sidewalk—clearly struggling, clearly in need.

People pass by. Eyes straight ahead.

They're in a hurry. They're unsure. Maybe they're afraid.

Maybe they're thinking, *"Someone else will stop."*

Now imagine you're the one standing still, watching.
What do you do?

Jesus once told a story that begins in a moment like this.

A man is traveling the dangerous road from **Jerusalem to Jericho**—a route known for its twists, turns, and hidden places where robbers could strike. And that's precisely what happens. He's ambushed. Beaten and stripped and left for dead on the side of the road.

As he lies helpless, **two respected men pass by**—a **priest** and a **Levite**, religious leaders. People expected to care.

But they don't stop. They cross to the other side. They walk on.

Then, a third traveler appears.

A **Samaritan**.

To Jesus' Jewish audience, this would've been *the least likely hero*. Samaritans were viewed as outsiders—despised, distrusted, even hated. But this man does something unexpected.

He *stops*.

He kneels beside the wounded man. Cleans his wounds. Bandage them.

Then he lifts him onto his donkey, carries him to an inn, and **pays for his recovery** with his own money and a promise to return if more is needed.

He doesn't ask, *"What did this guy do to get here?"*

He doesn't wonder, *"Is this my responsibility?"*

He **sees a human being** and responds with compassion.

Crossing the Divide

The Samaritan's kindness isn't just radical.

It's **revolutionary**.

In a world where people were expected to stick with their kind, he **steps across boundaries**—cultural, racial, and religious.

He doesn't ask if the man is like him.

He chooses to *be a neighbor*, not in **label**, but in **action**.

And Jesus? He ends the story with a challenge.

He doesn't ask:

"Who is your neighbor?"

He flips it:

"Which of these was a neighbor?"

The answer isn't in the background.

It's in **behavior**.

Living the Message Today

This story still challenges us.

We live in a world divided by differences—race, class, gender, religion, politics, and more.

It's easy to stay silent.

It's easy to assume someone else will step in.

It's easy to say, *"That's not my problem."*

But what if you're **called to be the one who stops**?

Being a neighbor today might look like this:

- Sitting with someone alone at lunch.

- Speaking up when you see bullying or discrimination.

- Listening to someone's story, especially when it challenges your assumptions, can be a powerful experience.

- Sharing your time, your attention, your resources—even when it's inconvenient.

- Advocating for someone whose voice isn't being heard.

Compassion isn't passive. It's a choice.

And the world needs more people who choose love over comfort.

Presence over avoidance.

Justice over indifference.

Pause & Reflect

- Is there someone in your school, church, or community who feels left out or overlooked?

- What would it look like to "cross the road" for them—to show up, speak up, or help in a real way?

One last thing to remember:

Being a neighbor isn't about who someone is; it's about who they are. It's about who you choose to be.

Start Small, Think Big

You don't have to change the world overnight.

But you *can* start with one person.

That's how justice begins—not with massive platforms or viral moments, but with everyday decisions to do what's right, even when it's quiet. Look for opportunities in your school, your church, and your neighborhood.

Volunteer. Speak up. Sit with someone new.

Be kind to the person who's hardest to love.

Get curious about people who are different from you—in background, in culture, in opinion.

Because when you start with **compassion**, understanding follows.

And when enough people choose **empathy over apathy, the atmosphere around us begins to shift.**

Pharaoh's Daughter: Quiet Courage in the Face of Injustice

(*Exodus 2:1–10*)

Not all heroes wear armor or lead armies. Some change the world with a single, compassionate decision—even when no one else is watching.

Pharaoh's daughter isn't the first person you think of when you imagine bravery.

She was royalty, living in the lap of luxury while her father ruled Egypt with an iron fist. And part of that rule? A horrifying law: every Hebrew baby boy was to be thrown into the Nile River. No exceptions. No mercy.

One day, while bathing in the river, Pharaoh's daughter spotted something strange among the reeds: a basket. Inside it? A crying baby. A Hebrew baby.

She knew exactly what this meant.

She also knew what the law demanded.

But something stirred in her heart.

Instead of looking away, instead of calling for a guard, she reached into the water and pulled the child into her arms. This was not what anyone expected from a member of the ruling class. It wasn't just an act of curiosity. It was an act of defiance—a decision to choose compassion over cruelty.

This small, quiet act, seemingly insignificant in the grand scheme of things, changed everything. It's a reminder that even the smallest acts of kindness and courage can have a ripple effect, shaping the course of history.

The baby in that basket was Moses—the one who would one day stand up to Pharaoh, lead the Israelites out of slavery, part the Red Sea, and receive the Ten Commandments. But none of that would have happened without a moment of mercy from a woman who had every reason to follow the rules and every power to ignore his cries.

And here's what's powerful: she didn't know the future. She didn't know who he'd become. It was a leap of faith, a decision made in the present without the certainty of what it might lead to.

She didn't know who he'd become.

She just knew he was a child in danger—and she chose to act.

Pharaoh's daughter reminds us that courage doesn't always look like shouting or fighting. Sometimes, it seems like a quiet "yes" when everyone else expects silence. It's doing the right thing, not for recognition, but because your heart won't let you walk away.

Perhaps you're not in a palace or facing a royal decree, but you're surrounded by moments that require quiet courage—such as speaking up for someone being mistreated, standing up to a bully, including someone who feels invisible, refusing to laugh at a cruel joke, or standing by your values when it would be easier to blend in.

The world doesn't need more people who follow the crowd. It requires more people like Pharaoh's daughter—those willing to act with compassion, even when it costs them something. You, too, have the potential to make a difference in the lives of others through your acts of courage and compassion.

Because you never know what kind of future your kindness might unlock.

Pause & Reflect

- Have you ever witnessed something unfair or unkind but weren't sure how to respond?

- What's one way you could show courage through compassion this week?

One last thing to remember:

Even small, quiet bravery can change the course of someone's life, including yours.

***

Amos' Voice: Justice for the Oppressed

(Read it in the Book of Amos, especially chapters 5–6)

Imagine being an ordinary person—no title, no followers, no platform—just someone who takes care of sheep and picks fruit from trees.

That was **Amos**.

He wasn't a professional prophet. He wasn't trained in theology or respected in religious circles. He was a **farmer** from the countryside—someone who probably never imagined himself calling out kings and confronting priests.

But when he saw **injustice flooding the land**, he could no longer stay silent.

God gave him a message—and he spoke.

Seeing Beyond the Surface

On the outside, Israel appeared to be thriving during the time of Amos.

The economy was thriving.

Temples were busy with worship.

Festivals were happening.

People took pride in their spiritual image.

But underneath? The **rich were exploiting the poor**.

Leaders could be bribed.

Justice was for sale.

And **those in power ignored the cries of the vulnerable.**

It was a society full of noise, but lacking **heart.**

That's where Amos stepped in.

He didn't sugarcoat the message. He didn't try to win approval.

He said what needed to be said:

"Let justice roll on like a river, righteousness like a never-failing stream." (Amos 5:24)

It wasn't just poetic.

It was a **wake-up call.**

God didn't want empty songs or impressive rituals.

He wanted a **heart that sees the hurting and acts on their behalf.**

Justice Is More Than a Hashtag

Amos' challenge still echoes today.

We live in a world where **inequality is a reality** in education, healthcare, safety, and opportunities. Some voices are still ignored. Some groups are still marginalized. Some systems still benefit the powerful and punish the weak.

And in every generation, **truth-tellers rise.**

Some speak through protests.

Some through social media.

Some through everyday courage—in classrooms, workplaces, and dinner tables.

Like Amos, you don't need credentials to care.

You need **compassion**—and **the courage to speak up**.

Where to Begin

Justice doesn't always start big.

It starts with **noticing**.

– Who's always left out at school?

– Are there policies or patterns in your community that don't treat people fairly?

– Do your own biases ever shape how you treat someone?

Start small, but **start**.

- Include someone who's often excluded.

- Volunteer with a group helping people in need.

- Have honest conversations about race, disability, or other forms of inequality.

- Challenge unfair jokes or stereotypes—even when it's uncomfortable.

You won't fix everything. But you're not meant to.

You're meant to do **something**.

When you use your voice—especially when it costs you comfort—you carry on the legacy of prophets like Amos.

Pause & Reflect

- Where in your world is something unfair, but everyone's pretending it's fine?

- How could you be a voice for change, even in a small way?

One last thing to remember:

You don't need a microphone to be a prophet.

You need a heart that breaks for what breaks God's—and a voice that's willing to speak.

***

Jesus and the Tax Collectors: Breaking Stereotypes

(See Matthew 9:9–13 and Luke 19:1–10)

Picture a crowd packed tight along a dusty road—everyone craning to get a glimpse of the man people whispered about. **Jesus.**

He could've gone to the respected leaders or the influencers in the room.

Instead? He **walked straight toward someone everyone avoided:**

A tax collector.

The Most Hated Job in Town

In Jesus' day, tax collectors weren't just disliked—they were **despised**.

They worked for the Roman Empire, which meant they were seen as traitors to their people.

Worse? Many abused their power, taking more than they were entitled to and pocketing the rest.

People saw them as **greedy, dishonest, and beyond saving**.

But Jesus didn't.

***

Matthew's Story

Matthew was sitting at his booth, collecting taxes. To most people walking by, he wasn't just ignored—he was hated. A Jewish man working for the Roman Empire? That made him a traitor in their eyes.

And not just any traitor—a greedy one.

Tax collectors were notorious for taking more than they needed and pocketing the extra. So Matthew wasn't just disliked for his job—he was seen as dishonest, selfish, and beyond saving.

He probably felt it, too. The side-eyes. The hushed insults. The shame of being excluded from his community.

But then Jesus walked up to his booth—and did something no one expected.

He didn't spit.

He didn't shame.

He didn't preach.

He said:

"Follow me."

And just like that, Matthew got up.

He left the booth.

Left the money.

Left the reputation he had built, however messy it was.

It was bold. Risky. Wild.

But he did it.

And that was just the beginning.

Later, Matthew threw a dinner party for Jesus, not with religious leaders or respected guests, but with people like himself: other tax collectors and those considered "sinners." The kind of folks society gave up on.

And Jesus didn't just show up—He sat down. He ate with them. He talked with them. Treated them like they mattered.

People watching were shocked. "Why is Jesus eating with *them*?"

But Jesus made it clear:

He came for the outcasts, not the already accepted.

For the sick, not the healthy.

For the ones that everyone else tries to forget.

And here's what's incredible—Matthew, the one people tried to write off, ended up writing one of the four Gospels. **The book of Matthew.** His words have helped generations know who Jesus is. A man no one believed in was trusted with telling the story of the Savior.

***

Zacchaeus's Story

Then there was **Zacchaeus**—wealthy, short, curious.

He couldn't see through the crowd, so he **climbed a tree**. That might sound silly, but it showed just how **desperate** he was to be seen.

And Jesus did see him.

"Zacchaeus, come down. I'm staying at your house today."

Everyone was stunned.

Why Zacchaeus? Why eat with *him*?

But Jesus wasn't there to impress the crowd.

He was there to reach the **forgotten**, the **misunderstood**, the **unloved**.

Zacchaeus, moved by grace, gave away half his wealth and promised to repay everyone he'd wronged.

A moment of kindness sparked a life of transformation.

Breaking the Mold Today

Jesus didn't stay safe or comfortable.

He stepped across social lines to **restore dignity** and **rewrite labels**.

And that invitation continues.

Stereotypes still exist—about people's looks, culture, past, gender, income, accent, disability, and clothes.

We judge *fast*, often without realizing it.

But Jesus calls us to slow down.

To *see*.

How to Start?

- Be curious before you judge.
- Ask about someone's story.
- Listen more than you speak.
- Sit with someone different.
- Celebrate cultures and voices beyond your own.

Breaking stereotypes doesn't just free others—it frees *you*, too.

It helps you become someone who **loves like Jesus**, not just in belief but in action.

Pause & Reflect

- Is there someone you've labeled before, really knowing them?

- What would change if you saw them the way Jesus sees them?

One last thing to remember:

You don't have to agree with someone's choices to value their humanity.

Love doesn't require comfort—it just requires courage.

***

The Widow's Mite: Sacrificial Giving and Generosity

(Read it in Luke 21:1–4 and Mark 12:41–44)

In the heart of the crowded temple courts, people gathered—some to pray, others to give. The offering boxes stood where everyone could see them, and many wealthy people arrived in fine robes, dropping in large sums of money with visible pride. The clink of coins echoed loudly. It was a display of generosity, and the onlookers took notice.

But **Jesus noticed something different**.

A poor widow crept through the crowd. No robe. No fanfare. Just two small coins in her hand—**the smallest currency** in all of Israel. She didn't try to get anyone's attention. She slipped the coins into the offering box and walked away.

No one else reacted.

But Jesus **stopped everything** to point her out.

"Truly I tell you," He said, "this poor widow has put in more than all the others. They gave out of their wealth, but she, out of her poverty, gave all she had to live on."

(Luke 21:3–4)

To the world, her gift was nearly invisible. But to Jesus?

It thundered with meaning.

She gave not from her surplus but from her **faith**.

Not from abundance but from **trust**.

It wasn't about the size of her offering—it was about the **depth of her devotion**.

The widow wasn't trying to impress anyone.

She was expressing love, courage, and surrender.

What Does Generosity Look Like?

Today, generosity is often tied to status—donating big, going viral, gaining applause. However, the widow's story completely flips that mindset. Jesus didn't honor the most significant donation. He honored the one who came with **the biggest heart**.

And it begs a question: *What are you willing to give when no one is watching?*

Generosity might look like:

- Sharing your lunch with someone who forgot theirs.

- Giving time to help a classmate study.

- Donating your favorite jacket, not just the one you never wear.

- Volunteering on a Saturday when you'd rather sleep in.

These are today's widow's mites—gifts that seem small but cost something personal, offered in love.

Pause & Reflect

- What's one way you've given—even just a little—that felt meaningful?

- Is there something you've been holding back out of fear or comfort?

One last thing to remember:

It's not about how much you give—it's about how much love you give it with.

***

The Early Church: Unity in Diversity

(See Acts 2 and Acts 15)

Imagine a room filled with people from all over the world—speaking different languages, representing diverse cultures, and sharing unique stories—suddenly able to understand each other. Not because they learned a new language but because **God made the connection possible.**

That was the day of **Pentecost** when the Holy Spirit came upon Jesus' followers. Flames of fire appeared over their heads, and they began speaking in languages they didn't know—**but others did**.

It was more than a miracle of speech.

It was a **miracle of unity**.

A New Kind of Community

The early church was like nothing the world had ever seen.

Jews and Gentiles.

Rich and poor.

Men and women.

Locals and foreigners.

All of them came together to form **a new kind of family**, built not on sameness but on **shared faith** in Jesus.

They met at home.

They broke bread.

They sold possessions to meet each other's needs.

They **lived radically different lives** together.

And while they didn't always agree, they stayed committed to **listening, loving, and learning from one another**.

The Big Decision: Who Belongs?

As the church grew, challenges came.

Some early leaders believed that to follow Jesus, everyone needed to follow traditional Jewish laws, like circumcision or dietary rules.

But others, like Paul and Barnabas, saw that **God's grace was bigger than one culture**. They believed that anyone could follow Jesus, regardless of their background.

So, the leaders held a council in Jerusalem. And after prayer and discussion, they made a bold decision: **Faith in Jesus—not following all the old laws—was what brought people into the family of God.**

That moment changed everything.

It opened the door wide for the entire world.

A Message for Today

We still live in a world full of differences.

Different languages.

Different styles.

Different opinions.

Different traditions.

And sometimes those differences **divide** us.

But the early church shows a better way.

A way of **unity without uniformity**.

You don't have to agree on every detail to **build something meaningful together**. You need **love, humility, and a shared mission**.

What Does That Look Like Now?

- Invite someone different from you into your friend group.

- Ask questions instead of assuming you know someone's story.

- Choose kindness over cliques.

- Celebrate cultural events or traditions different from your own.

- Step in when you see someone being left out or mistreated.

The early church wasn't perfect, but it was powerful because they chose **love over labels**.

And we can, too.

Pause & Reflect

- Are there people around you who feel invisible or excluded?

- What would it look like to help them feel like they belong?

One last thing to remember:

True unity doesn't erase differences—it welcomes them.

When we walk in love, we reflect the heart of God.

And together, we can build a community that bears a striking resemblance to heaven.

***

When Justice Calls: A Final Word from Chapter 5

Justice isn't just a word on a poster.

It's not just a debate topic in class or a buzzword on your social feed. Justice is *personal*. It's how you respond when you see someone being excluded. It's what you do when a friend is mistreated. It's the voice you choose to raise—or the silence you decide to break—when something's wrong.

And here's the truth:

The call to justice isn't only for politicians, pastors, or protest leaders.

It's for *you*.

The Good Samaritan showed us that genuine compassion transcends boundaries that others are too afraid to cross. He didn't look away. He moved toward the pain, and that made all the difference.

Pharaoh's daughter defied injustice not with protests, but with quiet courage. She rescued a life, not knowing the future, just knowing it was right.

Amos, a farmer with no platform, stood up and called out corruption. His boldness reminds us that truth doesn't require a title, just conviction.

Jesus, by spending time with tax collectors and outcasts, shattered stereotypes and redefined what it means to be a part of something.

Matthew, a man everyone avoided, was invited into Jesus' inner circle. Grace saw potential in someone others had already written off.

Zacchaeus climbed a tree to see Jesus and came down a changed man. One act of kindness led to a ripple of transformation.

The widow with two coins gave everything, even when no one noticed. Her gift was small in size, but massive in meaning.

The early church showed us that unity doesn't mean sameness. It means choosing love across all kinds of differences and sticking together even when it's hard

So, what does *justice* look like in your world?

It's not always a courtroom or a protest sign.

It's the moment you decide to:

- **Speak up** when someone's being bullied.

- **Push back** against unfair stereotypes.

- **Celebrate** a classmate's culture instead of mocking it.

- **Notice** who's sitting alone—and sit beside them.

- **Ask questions** when something doesn't feel right.

- **Give generously**, even if it's just your time or attention.

- **Refuse to laugh** at the joke that tears someone down.

These aren't dramatic moves.

They're *daily decisions*—and they matter more than you think.

You Can't Fix Everything... But You Can Do Something

You weren't meant to carry the weight of the whole world.

But you were created to reflect God's heart in the corner of the world you *do* touch.

That might be:

- Your school hallway.

- Your group chat.

- Your social media posts.

- Your dinner table.

- Your church youth group.

- Or the friend who trusts you with their most complex story.

In all those spaces, you can show up with empathy, with courage, and with a willingness to say, *"That's not okay, and I care enough to do something about it."*

Pause & Reflect

- Where do you see injustice—even in small ways—in your daily life?

- What's one way you could respond with compassion or courage this week?

One Last Thing to Remember:

You don't have to be loud to be bold. You don't have to be perfect to make a difference. And you don't need a spotlight to live with justice. When you show up with compassion, speak with truth, and act with integrity.

You're not just reacting to the world; you're helping rewrite it.

Looking Ahead: Embracing Growth, Even When It's Messy

You don't wake up one day completely transformed.

Growth isn't instant; it's often uncomfortable, uncertain, and slower than you want it to be. But every step matters.

In the next chapter, we dive into the kind of transformation that doesn't happen in a spotlight, but in quiet, honest moments with God. You'll meet people who changed directions after hitting rock bottom:

- Like **Saul**, whose life flipped from persecutor to preacher.

- Wrestled with identity and came out stronger like **Jacob**, who fought for a blessing.

- Asked hard questions and received honest answers, just like the **Samaritan woman** who met Jesus at a well and was forever changed.

- Carried deep regrets like **Peter**, who failed big but found redemption even bigger.

- They were seen in their suffering like the **man born blind**, whose healing revealed more than sight.

- Choose praise over fear like **Mary**, who responded to God's call with a song of faith and surrender.

These aren't stories of perfect people. They're stories of people who, despite feeling unworthy, unqualified, or unsure, were courageous enough to show up. Because transformation doesn't require perfection. It just requires openness.

As you read, think about this:

Where in your life is God inviting you to grow?

What part of your story is still being written?

And how could grace be shaping you, even now, providing comfort and support in your journey of growth?

Let's step into Chapter 6 together and discover what real growth looks like from the inside out.

Embracing Personal Growth and Transformation

Imagine this:

You're standing in the middle of a crowded hallway—everyone seems to know exactly who they are and where they're going. They're confident. Collected. Moving with purpose.

And you?

You're standing still, caught somewhere between who you *used* to be and who you *hope* to become.

That space—the *in-between*—can feel confusing and frustrating.

But it's also where **growth begins**.

From Persecutor to Preacher: The Story of Saul

(*Found in Acts 7–9*)

Before he became the Apostle Paul, he was **Saul**—a passionate Pharisee who believed he was doing the right thing by attacking the early followers of Jesus. He thought he was protecting the truth. In reality, he was running straight into a **wake-up call**.

When Stephen—the first Christian martyr—was stoned to death, Saul stood by, approving. That moment didn't convict him. It motivated him.

He got permission from the high priest to hunt down more Christians in Damascus. With righteous fury and letters of authority in his hands, Saul set out to **stop what he thought was wrong**.

But God had other plans.

A Collision with Grace

On the road to Damascus, **a blinding light** stopped him in his tracks. Saul fell to the ground and heard a voice:

"Saul, Saul, why are you persecuting me?" (Acts 9:4)

It was Jesus.

And in that moment, everything changed.

He was blinded—physically and spiritually. The man who had felt so powerful now had to be led by the hand into the city. For three days, he sat in darkness—fasting, praying, likely wrestling with everything he thought he knew.

And then, **God sent Ananias**.

Imagine the courage that it took. Ananias knew Saul's reputation, yet he obeyed God's call and stepped toward the man who had once hunted his friends.

He laid his hands on Saul and said:

"Brother Saul, the Lord Jesus... has sent me so that you may see again and be filled with the Holy Spirit." (Acts 9:17)

Suddenly, *something like scales* fell from Saul's eyes.

He could see.

He was baptized.

He was changed.

Transformation Takes Time—but It Starts with a Yes

Paul didn't become a spiritual giant overnight. He had to unlearn old ways of thinking. He had to rebuild trust with those who had previously feared him. He faced rejection, persecution, and hardship. But through it all, **he didn't turn back**.

He traveled across cities and continents, planting churches, mentoring believers, and writing letters that would become foundational to the New Testament.

He spoke boldly but always with humility, knowing what he had been saved from.

"If anyone is in Christ, they are a new creation. The old has gone; the new is here." (2 Corinthians 5:17)

That wasn't just a quote.

It was **Paul's reality**.

What Does This Mean for You?

Perhaps you can relate to Saul, driven by something that once felt right but now feels off.

Maybe you're in that **"three days of darkness"**—the waiting, the questioning, the wondering.

Or maybe you're like Ananias—unsure if someone like *you* could make a difference in someone else's story.

Wherever you are, here's what Paul's story tells us:

- **You're never too far gone to change.**

- **Even confusion can be the start of clarity.**

- **You don't have to see the whole path—take the next right step.**

Try This: Starting Your Transformation

- **Get honest.**

What's holding you back? A habit? A mindset? A fear of not being enough? Could you write it down? Name it.

- **Get quiet.**

Set aside time to pause and listen. Pray. Reflect. Read a Bible passage, such as Acts 9 or 2 Corinthians 5.

- **Get help.**

Growth doesn't happen alone. Consult with a mentor, youth leader, or trusted adult who can offer guidance and support throughout your journey.

- **Get moving.**

You don't need a lightning bolt moment to begin. Just start. One small decision can spark massive change.

Pause & Reflect

- What's one area of your life that needs a reset?

- If you believed fundamental transformation was possible, what would you do differently?

One Last Thing to Remember:

God doesn't just call the ready. He prepares the willing. And sometimes, the most powerful stories come from the most unlikely people.

Paul's journey wasn't smooth. But it was *real*.

So is yours.

This is your Damascus road.

This is your beginning.

Take the next step—and trust that God can do something incredible with your life.

Jacob's Ladder: Wrestling with Identity and Change

(*Genesis 25–33*)

Jacob's story is messy—in the most relatable way. It's about rivalry, mistakes, second chances, and the slow, sacred work of becoming someone new.

From the moment of his birth, Jacob was in a struggle. He came into the world clutching the heel of his twin brother Esau, already fighting for a place, for approval, for identity. That craving followed him into adulthood. He tricked Esau out of his birthright with a bowl of stew. Later, he dressed up like Esau—faking his voice, wearing goat skins to mimic his brother's hairy arms—and fooled their nearly blind father into giving him the blessing that wasn't meant for him.

He got what he wanted.

But he lost peace in the process.

Esau's rage sent Jacob running. He fled to his uncle Laban's house, hoping to leave the past behind. But there, the deceiver met deception. After working seven years to marry Rachel, he woke up to find Leah beside him, tricked into marrying the wrong sister. The irony was unmistakable: Jacob, the schemer, had been out-schemed.

Still, he persevered—building a family, accumulating wealth, and becoming someone others looked up to. However, the identity crisis still lingered inside. Was he the trickster? The runaway? The chosen heir? He couldn't run forever.

The Dream That Interrupted Everything

One night, sleeping in the wilderness with nothing but a rock for a pillow, Jacob had a dream. A ladder stretched from earth to heaven, with angels ascending and descending. At the top, God spoke:

"I am with you... I will not leave you." (*Genesis 28:15*)

This wasn't just a comforting moment—it was a spiritual wake-up call. Jacob, the one who schemed and ran, was being *seen* by the God of Abraham and Isaac. God wasn't distant. He was personal. And he had a purpose for Jacob's life.

But growth doesn't come overnight.

Years later, Jacob prepared to return home and face Esau. He was terrified. Unsure. He sent gifts ahead to soften his brother's anger. He prayed. He panicked.

Then came the moment that would change everything.

The Wrestle and the Rename

Alone in the dark, Jacob encountered a mysterious figure—some say an angel, others say it was God Himself. They wrestled until dawn.

This wasn't a dream. It was physical. Emotional. Spiritual.

Jacob refused to let go. "I *won't release you until you bless me,*" he gasped.

That fight—long, raw, and exhausting—left him with a limp. But it also left him **renamed**.

"You will no longer be Jacob, but Israel—because you have wrestled with God and with humans and have overcome." (*Genesis 32:28*)

That name change wasn't about the image. It was about identity. Jacob had faced himself—his fears, his past, his God—and emerged changed. He wasn't the deceiver anymore. He was someone transformed by the struggle.

The next day, when he met Esau, he didn't find vengeance. He found grace. Esau ran to him, embraced him, and wept. Years of tension melted in a single act of forgiveness.

Pause & Reflect

- What part of your identity have you been wrestling with lately?

- Where might God be meeting you in the struggle, not to punish, but to transform?

One Last Thing to Remember:

Wrestling doesn't mean you're failing—it means you're growing. God can meet you right in the struggle and turn it into your turning point.

***

The Woman at the Well: Breaking Free from the Past

(John 4:1–30)

She came to the well at noon, when the sun was at its hottest, and the town was quiet.

Most women fetched water in the early morning. But she came alone, carrying more than just a jar. She carried shame. Regret. The sting of being whispered about, avoided, misunderstood.

She didn't expect anyone to be there. But Jesus was.

And instead of ignoring her, He spoke:

"Will you give me a drink?"

With that one question, He shattered the cultural rules of the day. Jews didn't speak to Samaritans. Men didn't initiate conversation with unaccompanied women. Rabbis didn't engage with people considered "sinful." Yet here He was—asking, listening, seeing.

When the Past No Longer Defines You

Jesus didn't dodge her truth. He named it with gentleness:

"You've had five husbands, and the man you're with now isn't your husband." (John 4:18)

She didn't deny it. She didn't run.

Why? Because there was no judgment in His voice—only *invitation.*

Jesus offered her **living water**—a fresh start. Not based on what she had done but on *who she could become.*

And her response? She left her water jar—the very reason she came—and ran back to her village to tell everyone:

"Come see a man who told me everything I ever did... and still talked to me." (John 4:29, paraphrased)

Your Mistakes Are Not the End

She wasn't a religious scholar. She didn't have it all together. But her honesty became her testimony. The same woman who avoided people became the reason others came to Jesus.

Because she wasn't perfect, she was transformed.

That's what grace does—it doesn't erase your past, but it rewrites your future.

Pause & Reflect

- What would it look like to stop hiding your story and start sharing it?

- What "jar" do you need to lay down to walk forward?

One Last Thing to Remember:
God doesn't flinch at your truth. He sees every part of your story—the regrets, the heartbreak, the silence—and still leans in with love. You are not too far gone. You are not too broken. You are deeply known... and still deeply wanted. That's the kind of love that heals what shame tried to bury—and brings you back to life.

★★★

Peter's Redemption: Overcoming Failures

(*Matthew* 26:69–75; John 21:1–19; Acts 2)

Picture a dim courtyard under the cover of night—the fire crackles, casting long shadows while tension hangs thick in the air. Peter lingers nearby, watching the unthinkable unfold—his beloved teacher arrested, mocked, and beaten. Just hours before, Peter had boldly promised, "*Even if everyone else falls away, I won't.*" (Matthew 26:33)

But now, fear takes over.

When people recognize him and ask, "*Weren't you with Jesus?*" he panics—not once, not twice, but three times. "*I don't know Him,*" he insists. And then..

The rooster crows.

That sound slices through the silence like a knife. And suddenly, Peter remembers Jesus' warning: "***Before the rooster crows, you will disown me three times.***" (Matthew 26:34)

Shame crashes down. His confidence evaporates. He runs—broken and undone.

Peter had believed in his loyalty. His love for Jesus was real. But fear exposed a weakness he hadn't seen in himself. As Jesus is led to the cross, Peter carries more than grief—he carries guilt, the kind that makes you question your identity, your worth, and whether you still belong.

But Peter's story doesn't end there.

A Beach, a Fire, and a Question

After the resurrection, Jesus appears to His disciples at the Sea of Galilee. It's a quiet, simple scene: breakfast on the beach. Fish cooking over a fire. And Peter—still carrying that failure—sits across from the very one he betrayed.

Jesus looks at him and asks, "***Do you love me?***"

Three times.

Once for each denial.

But instead of shame, Jesus offers purpose: "**Feed my sheep**." (John 21:15-17)

This isn't punishment—it's restoration.

Jesus is saying:

I know what you did. I still choose you. Let's rebuild together.

That moment reshapes everything.

After that encounter, Peter changes. The same man who once denied Jesus out of fear now stands before a crowd in Jerusalem and boldly proclaims the gospel at Pentecost (Acts 2).

Thousands believe. Miracles follow. The early church grows.

Peter doesn't lead from perfection. He leads from grace. He knows what it's like to fall hard and be picked back up. His failure didn't disqualify him. It became his testimony.

That's redemption.

That's what God does with our worst moments. He doesn't erase them—He transforms them into strength.

What This Means for You

Maybe you've made mistakes that haunt you—said things you regret. Walked away from someone you care about. Perhaps you feel like your failure has written the end of your story.

Peter's story says otherwise.

- *Failure isn't final when grace steps in.*

- *You're not disqualified—you're being refined.*

- *God doesn't discard broken people. He builds with them.*

You don't have to be perfect to move forward. You have to be willing to say yes when Jesus asks, **"Do you love Me?"**

Peter's transformation reminds us:

- You are more than your worst moment.

- Redemption is real.

- Grace is available.

- And your most significant influence may come from the place you once thought disqualified you.

You're not finished.

This is where healing begins.

This is where your boldness is born.

So go ahead—stand back up. Jesus is calling you to lead from a place of grace.

Pause & Reflect

- Have you ever felt like a mistake defined you? What would change if you believed God could redeem it?

- What's one step you can take today toward healing or reconciliation?

One Last Thing to Remember:

God doesn't cancel people who mess up. He restores them. So even if you've failed, you're not finished. Let grace rewrite your story.

***

The Blind Man's Sight: Seeing Beyond Limitations

(John 9:1–38)

Picture the crowded streets of ancient Jerusalem—the noise, the dust, the shuffle of feet, and the swirl of cloaks. People move with purpose. Most barely notice the man sitting at the edge of the path. He's been there for years—blind from birth, unseen by many, known only by his limitations.

To the crowds, he's just *that* beggar.

To the disciples, he becomes a question:

"Rabbi, who sinned, this man or his parents, that he was born blind?"

But to Jesus, he's neither a problem to solve nor a punishment to explain.

He's a person to be seen.

Jesus responds with compassion and clarity:

"This happened so that the works of God might be displayed in him." (John 9:3)

Then Jesus does something unexpected.

He kneels. Spits in the dirt. Mixes mud.

And with gentle hands, he places it on the man's eyes.

"Go," He says, **"wash in the Pool of Siloam."**

There's no dramatic countdown.

No crowd cheering.

It's just a quiet act of obedience.

The man goes.

He washes.

And for the first time in his life, he sees.

Shapes. Light. Faces. Color. Movement. The world bursts open.

But the miracle doesn't end with sight.

It launches a mission.

Word spreads fast. The man is dragged in front of religious leaders. Questions fly. Accusations swirl. Some refuse to believe it's even the same man. Others press him for answers:

"How were your eyes opened?"

"Who did this?"

"Is He from God or not?"

But the man doesn't back down.

His answer cuts through the noise:

"One thing I do know: I was blind, but now I see." (John 9:25)

He doesn't have all the theological answers.

He doesn't pretend to be an expert.

He tells the truth.

And sometimes, that's the boldest thing you can do.

From Margins to Mission

Before the healing, he was sidelined.

After the healing, he became a witness.

Not because he fit the mold. Not because he had all the right words.

However, because he had undergone a profound transformation, he refused to remain silent about it.

Even when the leaders kicked him out of the synagogue, he stood his ground.

Later, Jesus found him again and revealed who He truly was—the Son of God. The man believed and worshiped.

His journey from darkness to light wasn't just physical; it was also spiritual.

It was personal. Spiritual. Complete.

What This Means for You

Perhaps you feel confined by your limitations—what others see *or* what you've come to believe about yourself.

Maybe you've been overlooked, underestimated, or misunderstood.

This story reminds you:

- God sees what others don't.

- Your limitations don't cancel your purpose.

- Your story has power—even if it doesn't fit what others expect.

- Your so-called weakness might be the place where God wants to showcase His strength.

You're Not Defined by What You Can't Do

The blind man didn't go looking for Jesus.

Jesus found *him*.

And He still finds us—right where we are. In our questions. In our limitations and our waiting.

So, take the next step.

Say yes when He calls.

And remember, transformation often begins not with what you see, but how you start to see *yourself*.

Pause & Reflect

- What "labels" have others placed on you—or you've put on yourself—that need to be rewritten?

- What would it look like to walk forward with faith, even if you don't have all the answers?

One Last Thing to Remember:

You don't need all the answers to make an impact. You just need the courage to say, "This is what God has done for me"—and let that light speak louder than any doubt.

***

Mary's Magnificat: Embracing Change with Joy

(Found in Luke 1:26–56)

Picture a quiet afternoon in a small village called Nazareth. The streets are dusty. The houses are humble. And in one of them sits a teenage girl named Mary—young, unknown, and likely planning a very everyday life. She's engaged to a man named Joseph. Maybe she's thinking about her future, her wedding, her dreams.

Then everything changes.

Suddenly, an angel appears—Gabriel, a messenger from heaven. His words are stunning:

"Greetings, you who are highly favored! The Lord is with you."

Mary is startled. Confused. She's never seen anything like this before. And what Gabriel says next shakes her world:

"You will conceive and give birth to a son, and you are to call him Jesus. He will be great... and his kingdom will never end." (Luke 1:31–33, paraphrased)

It's more than unexpected—it's overwhelming. Mary isn't married yet. She's just a teenager. How could this be happening?

She asks the only question that makes sense:

"How can this be?"

Gabriel explains that the Holy Spirit will come upon her—that this child will be the Son of God. It's divine. Miraculous. History-shifting.

Then comes the most remarkable part of the whole story.

Mary doesn't argue.

She doesn't ask for a backup plan.

She says:

"I am the Lord's servant. May your word to me be fulfilled." (Luke 1:38)

That "yes" changed everything.

A Visit that Confirms the Miracle

Not long after, Mary travels to visit her cousin Elizabeth, who is also miraculously pregnant, with a child who would become John the Baptist. As soon as Mary walks in, Elizabeth's baby leaps into her womb, and Elizabeth is filled with joy.

She exclaims:

"Blessed are you among women, and blessed is the child you will bear!"

In that moment, Mary's courage is affirmed. She's not alone. She's not imagining things. This is real—and it's holy.

What Mary does next is nothing short of powerful.

She lifts her voice in a song.

A song not of fear, but of **faith.**

The Magnificat: A Song of Bold Praise

Mary's song, now called the **Magnificat**, is recorded in Luke 1:46–55. It's not about her being special or perfect—it's about God's faithfulness. Her words are bold, beautiful, and justice-filled:

"My soul magnifies the Lord, and my spirit rejoices in God my Savior...

He has brought down rulers from their thrones but lifted the humble." (*Luke 1:46–55, selected*)

This teenage girl from a quiet village becomes the voice of something eternal. She celebrates not only what God is doing in her, but what God is doing in the world. Her song is a declaration that the overlooked matter is being addressed, that the poor are seen, and that change is coming.

Mary didn't have all the answers.

But she had trust.

And that trust gave her joy—absolute, rooted, unstoppable joy.

The Journey Ahead

Mary's "yes" didn't lead to an easy life. She carried Jesus in her womb. She raised Him. She watched Him teach, heal, and challenge the powerful. And she stood at the foot of the cross when He died—her heart shattered, yet still **faithful.**

She didn't always understand. But she stayed.

Her story is not just about one moment of bravery—it's about a lifetime of quiet strength.

What This Means for You

You may not be visited by an angel or asked to carry the Son of God, but you will face moments that change everything.

New schools.

Shifting friendships.

Family stress.

Big decisions that stretch you.

Change is hard. But it can also be **holy**.

Mary's story shows us that joy isn't found in having life perfectly figured out. It's found in saying yes to God, who already knows the way. She teaches us that courage often looks like surrender—and that surrender opens the door to something bigger than we could ever imagine.

Pause & Reflect

- What's one change in your life right now that feels scary—or sacred?

- If you trusted God like Mary did, how might that change your response to life?

Try This: Finding Joy in Uncertainty

Start a gratitude journal. Each day, write down one thing that made you smile, one thing that challenged you, and one thing you're hopeful for.

Over time, you'll begin to see how God is working—even in the unknown.

And surround yourself with "Elizabeths"—people who affirm you, support you, and remind you of who you are when you forget.

Final Thought

Mary's Magnificat was more than just a song.

It was a declaration of joy, justice, and faith in a God who turned the world upside down.

When you say yes to growth—even when it's messy or uncertain—you join that same song.

You become part of a story that is still unfolding.

So lift your voice.

Choose trust.

And embrace change—not with fear, but with joy.

One Last Thing to Remember

Mary didn't wait for perfect understanding—she trusted a perfect God. You don't need all the answers to move forward. Sometimes, your boldest "yes" is simply choosing joy in the middle of the unknown.

When Growth Feels Hard: A Final Word from Chapter 6

Growth isn't always dramatic. It's not always a big speech, a viral moment, or a lightning bolt of clarity. More often?

It's quiet.

Personal.

Messy.

It seems like wrestling with who you are and who you're becoming.

It feels like uncertainty—when your old habits no longer fit, but the new ones haven't yet taken shape. It sounds like whispered prayers and internal questions:

"Can I change?"

"Will people still accept me?"

"What if I fail again?"

And yet—**this is where transformation happens.**

Not in perfection, but in the *willingness* to keep going anyway.

Throughout this chapter, you've met people who stumbled.

Who doubted.

Who felt lost—and still said *yes* to becoming something more.

- **Saul became Paul**, turning from fierce opposition to passionate purpose.

- **Jacob ran from his past**, only to find identity and grace through struggle and reconciliation.

- **The Samaritan woman**, once shamed, found her voice and became a messenger of hope.

- **Peter denied Jesus** in fear, but grace rewrote his story and gave him the boldness to lead.

- **The blind man** gained more than sight—he discovered courage, purpose, and spiritual clarity.

- **Mary didn't just accept change**—she embraced it with joy and trust, letting her *eyes* change the course of history.

None of them had it easy.

None of them were perfect.

But they were *open*.

And that made all the difference.

Pause & Reflect

- Which story from this chapter spoke to you the most, and why?

- What fear, habit, or label might be holding you back from your growth?

- What would it look like for you to say "yes" to God in this season of your life?

Here's the truth:

You *will* change.

That's not a maybe. It's a guarantee.

Your thoughts will evolve.

Your dreams will shift.

Your heart will stretch in ways you never expected.

But how you grow—that part is up to you.

Will you harden? Or will you soften and stretch?

Will you run from transformation? Or lean into it?

You don't have to become someone completely different.

You need to become more *of who you* are—you, God created, gifted, and is gently shaping through every season.

One Last Thought

When growth feels hard, don't panic. Don't retreat. Just remember: every person in this chapter stood where you're standing now—unsure, unqualified, undone. And yet, **they continued to move forward.**

So when your identity feels shaky, when shame whispers lies, when the future looks like fog, don't wait for perfect clarity. Just give God your next step. The transformation doesn't need to be loud. It doesn't need a spotlight.

It just needs **your yes**.

Because, yes, that is where healing begins.

Yes, it is where shame breaks.

Yes, it is where purpose is born.

Your growth isn't random.

It's sacred.

And you're not alone on the journey.

Let's keep walking—together.

Looking Ahead: When Courage Feels Costly

Courage doesn't always come with a battle cry.

Sometimes, it seems like taking a step forward when no one else is willing to.

Sometimes, it's saying what's true, even when your voice shakes.

Sometimes, it's choosing to trust when the outcome is still unknown.

In this next chapter, we're going to look at what **real bravery** looks like—not the kind that's loud for attention, but the kind that stands firm under pressure.

You'll meet people who, like you, faced overwhelming odds, dangerous kings, fiery furnaces, and moments where everything was on the line.

Some were warriors. Some were protectors. Some were overlooked. And some were terrified—but they still showed up.

Because courage isn't about being fearless.

It's about moving forward, even when you're afraid. Your fear does not negate your courage; it only amplifies it.

In a world that often celebrates comfort and popularity, these stories remind us what it means to **stand for something more profound**—to live with integrity, boldness, and faith that never wavers.

So, if you've ever felt like the only one trying to do the right thing.

If you've ever faced a situation that made your heart race or your knees shake.

You're in good company.

Let's discover together how courage grows—not in the absence of fear, but right in the middle of it.

Cultivating Courage and Bravery

I magine standing at the edge of a cliff—your heart pounding, the wind tugging at your clothes, and a drop below that feels both terrifying and thrilling. That moment-the one right before you leap—is where bravery is born. Courage doesn't always mean feeling confident. Most of the time, it feels like a choice made out of fear.

One of the most iconic examples of courage in Scripture is the story of David and Goliath. But if you've only ever heard it as "the boy who beat the giant," you're missing the depth of what happened—and why it still matters for your life today.

David and Goliath: Courage That Comes from the Quiet Places

(1 Samuel 17)

David wasn't a soldier. He wasn't trained in battle. He wasn't even old enough to join the army. He was a shepherd boy—the youngest in his family, overlooked by his brothers and tasked with delivering lunch to the soldiers on the battlefield. When he arrived, he didn't expect to be pulled into a national crisis. But he saw one unfold right before him.

A Philistine warrior named Goliath—over nine feet tall and clad in heavy armor—was taunting the Israelite army. Day after day, he mocked them, daring anyone to fight him. And day after day, the warriors of Israel—including David's older brothers—froze in fear (1 Samuel 17:10-11).

But David? He saw something different. He didn't just see a giant—he saw an opportunity to trust God publicly, just as he had trusted Him privately. While watching sheep, David had fought off lions and bears (1 Samuel 17:34-36). No one had applauded those victories. No one even knew. But David remembered. In those quiet, lonely fields, God had been faithful. That was the courage he carried now.

When King Saul offered David his armor, David respectfully declined (1 Samuel 17:38-39). He didn't need someone else's weapons—he needed what had always worked: his faith, a sling, and five smooth stones. That's all. No sword. No shield. Just trust.

Standing before Goliath, David didn't tremble. Instead, he declared:

"You come against me with sword and spear and javelin, but I come against you in the name of the Lord Almighty... This day, the Lord will deliver you into my hands." —1 Samuel 17:45–46 (NIV)

Then, with one stone, one perfectly aimed throw, and one massive leap of faith, the impossible happened: the giant fell. David didn't just win a battle—he broke a spirit of fear that had gripped an entire nation.

The Real Source of Bravery

David's courage didn't come from self-confidence. It came from God-confidence. While others measured Goliath's size, David measured God's strength. That shift in focus changed everything. The story isn't about a boy defeating a giant. It's about how deep faith can lead to daring action.

But here's the part we often miss: David's bravery didn't begin on the battlefield. It started in the ordinary. In the mundane. In the lonely work of tending sheep, staying faithful, and practicing trust when no one was watching.

That's where real courage grows.

Facing Your Giants

You probably won't face a giant in armor, but you will face fears that feel just as overwhelming. It could be fear of failure, rejection, or not being good enough. Perhaps it's the anxiety of trying something new or standing alone when your values don't align with the crowd.

Those moments are your battlefield.

And like David, you have a choice: let fear rule you or let faith lead you.

You don't need a perfect plan or heroic confidence. You need to take one step forward with what you have. Your sling and stone might be a prayer. A conversation. A decision to speak up. A moment of silent trust when the world feels loud.

Why Your Courage Matters

David's bravery didn't just impact his life. It inspired a nation. That's the ripple effect of courage: it's contagious. Your boldness—however small it may seem—can give someone else the strength to face their fears.

So when you're standing at the edge of something hard, remember this: bravery isn't about being fearless. It's about moving forward with your faith louder than your fear.

And just like David, you don't have to be the biggest, the strongest, or the most experienced. You have to be willing.

Pause & Reflect

- What "giant" in your life feels impossible right now?

- Where have you seen God's faithfulness in the small things—moments that might be preparing you for something bigger?

One Last Thing to Remember:

Courage isn't built in the spotlight. It's built in a quiet place. In faith. In practice. In saying yes, again and again. Your giants may be big. But your God is bigger. Pick up your stone. Step into the valley. And trust that you are not alone.

***

Shadrach, Meshach, and Abednego: Standing Firm Under Fire

(Daniel 3)

Imagine this:

You're standing in a massive open field under the scorching sun, surrounded by thousands of people. Everyone is facing the same direction, staring at a 90-foot-tall golden statue towering over the crowd. Then, a royal announcement booms through the air:

"When the music plays, you must bow. Anyone who refuses will be thrown into a blazing furnace."

There's no negotiation. No second chances. Just a moment of pressure—and a choice.

That was the reality for three young men: **Shadrach, Meshach, and Abednego**. Teenagers like you. Exiles from Israel, now living in Babylon under the rule of King Nebuchadnezzar. They had already endured a great deal—new names, new culture, and new expectations. They had learned to adapt. But this command? This was a line they wouldn't cross.

As the music played and thousands of people hit the ground in submission, Shadrach, Meshach, and Abednego remained standing. They didn't yell. They didn't make a scene. They refused to bow.

Courage Isn't Always Loud

Their stand wasn't dramatic, but it was daring. In a world demanding compromise, they chose conviction.

When word reached the king, he was furious. He summoned the three and gave them a final chance. **Bow or burn.**

Their answer is one of the boldest declarations of faith in Scripture:

"If we are thrown into the blazing furnace, the God we serve can deliver us from it...

*****But even if He does not****, we want you to know, O king, that we will not serve your gods."*— Daniel 3:17–18 (NIV)

Their faith wasn't based on guaranteed outcomes. They didn't say, "We'll stand if God rescues us."

They said, **"We'll stand, no matter what."**

That's real courage—not knowing what comes next but still choosing to be faithful.

Fire That Frees

Enraged, King Nebuchadnezzar ordered the furnace to be heated seven times hotter than usual. It was so intense that the flames consumed the soldiers who threw the three men into the fire.

But something miraculous happened.

Inside that furnace, the king saw not three men, but four.

"Didn't we tie up three men and throw them into the fire?" he asked.

"Look! I see four men walking around unharmed. And the fourth looks like a son of the gods." — Daniel 3:24–25 (paraphrased)

Shadrach, Meshach, and Abednego weren't alone. **Jesus was with them in the fire.**

When they stepped out, not a single hair was singed. Their clothes weren't scorched. They didn't even smell like smoke..

The very fire that was supposed to destroy them?

It only burned off their ropes.

Standing When It's Easier to Bow

This story isn't just about supernatural protection—it's about spiritual resilience.

The courage to stand starts long before the flames. It's rooted in quiet decisions to follow God when no one's watching. Shadrach, Meshach, and Abednego weren't trying to make a statement. They were living by their convictions—faithfully, consistently, even when the stakes got high.

You may not face a golden statue or a blazing furnace, but you'll face moments that test your faith:

- When friends pressure you to go along with something that feels wrong.

- When speaking the truth might cost you popularity.

- When your beliefs feel out of place in your school or social circle.

In those moments, you'll feel the heat. But you'll also have a choice.

And here's the truth:

You're never standing alone. God doesn't meet you after the fire. He **joins you in it.** He walks with you under pressure, protects you in pain, and uses your courage to point others to Him, just like He did with these three brave young men.

Faith That Can't Be Burned

Shadrach, Meshach, and Abednego didn't know the end of the story when they made their stand. They didn't know if God would rescue them, but they stood anyway.

That's what true faith looks like.

Their story reminds us that bravery isn't about having power; it's about having the courage to act. It's about having **a presence**—God's presence with you in every challenge.

So when the world around you says "Bow," and you know in your heart that standing is the right thing to do, **stand.**

Quietly.

Boldly.

Faithfully.

Your fire moment may feel scary, but it might just become the place where you experience God most clearly.

And who knows?

Your stand might help someone else rise as well.

Pause & Reflect

- What situations in your life make it hard to stand for what's right?

- What would it look like to trust God even when the outcome is uncertain?

One Last Thing to Remember:

Courage isn't always loud. Sometimes it's a quiet stand when everyone else bows. You won't face a furnace—but you will face pressure. And when you do, remember: God is with you in it, not just after it. The fire won't define you. But your faith in the fire?

That just might.

***

Jehosheba's Hidden Bravery: Protecting a Future King

(2 Kings 11:1-3)

Before Israel had brave queens like Esther or mighty kings like David, there was someone quietly protecting the future in the shadows.

Her name was **Jehosheba**.

She didn't have a crown or command an army. She wasn't a prophet or a warrior. But what she did was nothing short of heroic.

The Crisis

It started with chaos. After the death of King Ahaziah, his mother, Queen Athaliah, seized power. She was ruthless. Determined to keep control, she did the unthinkable—ordered the execution of every male royal descendant, even her grandchildren.

It was a brutal plan to wipe out the royal family and secure her throne.

But in the shadows, one woman refused to let evil win.

Jehosheba, the sister of King Ahaziah and wife of Jehoiada, the priest, took a considerable risk. She rescued **Joash**, her baby nephew, from the slaughter.

With the help of her husband, she hid him and his nurse in a bedroom of the temple for six years.

Six years of secrecy. Six years of praying he wouldn't be found. Six years of trusting that God had a purpose.

A Hidden Rescue

Jehosheba's bravery wasn't loud or public. She didn't stand before crowds or face down enemies in battle. She made a quiet, behind-the-scenes decision to do what was right, even when it was dangerous.

She could've stayed silent. She could've followed orders. But she didn't.

She acted with conviction, risking her own life to protect an innocent one. And through her, God preserved the line of David—the same royal line that would one day lead to Jesus.

She didn't know the full impact of her choice. She just knew someone needed help, and she stepped in.

Think about it: without Jehosheba, Joash wouldn't have survived. Without Joash, the royal line might have ended. And without that royal line, the promise God made to David—the promise that led to Jesus—could've seemed broken. But

God used a woman whose name most people have never heard to protect that promise.

When Quiet Courage Changes Everything

Sometimes, we think bravery only counts if it's big—shouting the truth from a stage or standing in front of a crowd. But Jehosheba's story reminds us that some of the most powerful acts of courage happen when no one is watching. It's the small, quiet decisions to do what's right that can change the course of history.

It's standing up for someone vulnerable. It's choosing to protect rather than stay passive. It's doing the right thing—even when it's risky.

Maybe you've seen something that isn't right. Perhaps you've felt the urge to speak up or step in, but fear held you back.

You're not alone in that.

Jehosheba's story encourages us to act, even when we're not in the spotlight, even when the danger is real, and even when we're unsure of the outcome.

Because one act of courage—one "yes" to doing what's right—can ripple out further than you ever imagined.

Joash would eventually grow up to be king. And his reign brought reforms that led the people back to God. All of that happened because one woman said, "Not on my watch."

She chose life. She chose faith. She chose courage. Her unwavering faith in God's plan, even in the face of danger, is a testament to the power of belief. It serves as a reminder that our faith can be a source of strength and courage in the most challenging times.

And God used her in ways she never could've seen coming.

Her story is a challenge to each of us: **Don't underestimate your influence**. Even if you're not the loudest. Even if your role feels small, God sees. God knows. And He often uses the hidden heroes to do His most important work.

When You Feel Overlooked

Maybe you've felt like what you do doesn't matter, that no one notices when you do the right thing. That your quiet faithfulness is invisible.

But it's not.

God sees you. He sees your quiet acts of courage, your faithfulness, and your commitment to doing what's right. Just like He used Jehosheba in the middle of political chaos, family trauma, and personal danger, He can use you. Your actions, no matter how small they may seem, are part of a bigger story, and God sees their significance.

You may never be in a history book. But you could change someone's future just by stepping in when it matters most.

Pause & Reflect

- Have you ever witnessed something wrong and wondered whether you should speak up or take action?

- What does quiet courage look like in your life today? Could your decision to protect or support someone be part of a bigger story?

One last thing to remember:

You don't have to be famous to be faithful. You don't need a stage to be brave. Sometimes, God uses hidden heroes to protect His most excellent plans. Maybe you're one of them.

***

Joshua's Leadership: Stepping Boldly into the Unknown

Book of Joshua (especially chapters 1–6)

Picture this:

You're standing on the edge of something brand new. Behind you is the wilderness—years of wandering, waiting, and wondering. In front of you? A promise. A future filled with hope. But also fear. The unknown. A challenge that feels way bigger than you.

That's precisely where Joshua stood.

He wasn't new to leadership, but this was a different experience. For years, he had served as Moses' assistant. He had watched miracles unfold—plagues in Egypt, the parting of the Red Sea, manna falling from the sky. He had seen God provide and protect. But now Moses was gone. And all eyes were on Joshua.

He was the one God had chosen to lead the Israelites into the Promised Land.

It was a massive responsibility. And the moment wasn't just historical—it was deeply personal. How do you step into shoes that once stood on holy ground? How do you lead a people known for their complaining, their fear, and their forgetfulness?

Before Joshua took his first step forward, God gave him a command—and a promise:

"Be strong and courageous. Do not be afraid or discouraged, for the Lord your God will be with you wherever you go." (Joshua 1:9)

This wasn't just encouragement—it was marching orders from heaven. Strength and courage weren't optional. They were the foundation of Joshua's leadership. And they didn't come from self-confidence—they came from knowing God was with him.

The Battle That Didn't Make Sense

Not long after stepping into his new role, Joshua faced his first major test: *Jericho.*

Jericho was a fortified city with massive walls, strong gates, and a trained military force. It stood in the way of everything God had promised. But instead of giving Joshua a typical battle plan,

God gave him something completely unexpected.

March around the city once a day for six days.

On the seventh day, march around seven times.

Then blow trumpets and shout.

No swords. There are no surprise attacks. Just trust and obey.

Let's be honest—on paper, it probably looked ridiculous. Can you imagine how the Israelites felt on the third or fourth day? Marching quietly while the enemy looked down from the walls, probably laughing?

But Joshua didn't back down. He didn't ask God for a "better" plan. He led with calm determination. Because he knew something powerful: when God gives the plan, your job is to follow—even when it's weird, slow, or doesn't seem to be working.

On the seventh day, after that seventh lap, they shouted. And the walls-those giant, impenetrable walls—came crashing down.

No one saw it coming.

It wasn't just a military win. It was a **faith victory**. It proved that when you trust God with the impossible, He can do what no one else can.

Leading with Courage, Not Control

Joshua's strength wasn't in knowing everything. It was in listening. Trusting. Acting.

He had questions, sure. He felt the weight of leadership. But he kept coming back to the promise:

"The Lord your God is with you wherever you go."

That kind of leadership doesn't rely on charisma or perfection. It's about showing up. It's about being faithful. And when you lead in that manner, others take notice.

Joshua's boldness unified the tribes. It gave people hope. His steady trust became contagious. He showed what it means to be a leader who leans on God.

What This Means for You

You don't have to be standing in front of a walled city to feel overwhelmed. Life is full of moments that stretch you, where the next step feels unclear, and the pressure feels too big.

It could be being asked to lead a group project when you're unsure of your ideas.

It could be being the first to stand up for someone when everyone else is silent.

It may be navigating a family situation that feels way beyond your control.

Leadership starts small.

It begins with choosing courage when you'd rather stay quiet by helping others feel seen. Staying grounded in what's right—even when it's not easy.

You don't need a title. You need **willingness**. That's what God is looking for.

One Final Thought: You're Not Alone

Joshua didn't become a great leader overnight. He learned. He followed. He failed sometimes. But through it all, God stayed close.

The same is true for you.

You were created with purpose. And when you walk in courage—not because you feel brave, but because you trust the One who goes with you—you'll lead in a way that brings life, healing, and hope to those around you.

Leadership isn't about having the loudest voice in the room. It's about having a grounded heart.

So the next time you're standing at the edge of something unknown, do what Joshua did:

Take a deep breath.

Remember the promise.

And step forward in faith.

Pause & Reflect

- What's one area of your life where you feel called to step up, but feel unsure or afraid?

- Can you identify a "Jericho" you're facing right now—something that looks impossible without God's help?

- What would it look like to lead with courage, even if you don't have all the answers?

One Last Thing to Remember:

You don't need to have it all figured out. Just be willing to take the next step—because courage grows as you move, not before. God's not waiting at the finish line. He's walking with you into the unknown.

Rahab's Risk: Courage and Transformation

(Joshua 2, Joshua 6, and Matthew 1:5)

Imagine living in a city that's on edge. The gates are locked. Fear hangs in the air. People whisper about an unstoppable army marching closer by the day. Jericho, your home, is a fortress, famous for its towering walls and tight security. But even behind those walls, everyone's nervous. The Israelites are coming, and they've got a reputation for miracles—especially the God they follow.

This is the world in which Rahab lived.

She wasn't a queen or a soldier. She wasn't rich or famous. She was a woman with a rough reputation—a prostitute who lived in a house built into the city wall. Most people overlooked her. Others judged her. But when two Israelite spies arrived in Jericho on a secret mission, they didn't go to a palace or a guardhouse. They ended up at Rahab's door.

And Rahab let them in.

A Risk That Changed Everything

She could've turned them away. She could've reported them to the king. Instead, she hid them on her roof—under stalks of drying flax—knowing that if anyone found out, she could be killed for treason.

Why would she do something so risky?

Because Rahab *believed*.

She had heard the stories—the Red Sea splitting in two, the Israelites defeating powerful kings, the ways God had rescued and protected His people. She didn't grow up knowing God. But something in those stories told her He was real. And she decided to trust Him.

She told the spies,

"I know that the Lord has given you this land... the Lord your God is God in heaven above and on the earth below." *(Joshua 2:9–11, paraphrased)*

Think about that—Rahab was in a city full of people who feared Israel, but she was the only one who responded with faith.

The Scarlet Cord: A Sign of Trust

In exchange for protecting the spies, Rahab asked for one thing: that when Israel came to take Jericho, her family would be spared. The spies agreed. Their one instruction?

"Tie a scarlet cord in your window."*(Joshua 2:18)*

That scarlet cord wasn't just a piece of rope. It was a signal. A statement. A symbol of faith. While the rest of the city trembled, Rahab chose trust. She didn't know exactly how things would unfold. But she believed enough to act.

When the Israelites returned, and the walls of Jericho came crashing down, Rahab's house—right there on the wall—remained standing. Everyone inside was safe.

From the Edge to the Center of God's Story

But Rahab's story didn't stop there.

She joined the people of Israel. She didn't go back to her old life. She stepped into something entirely new. Eventually, she married a man named Salmon and became the great-great-grandmother of King David. And if that wasn't amazing enough, her name shows up in the family tree of Jesus Himself (Matthew 1:5).

Think about that: a woman with a painful past, overlooked by society, became part of the lineage of the Savior of the world. All because she believed—and acted on that belief.

What Rahab's Story Teaches Us

Rahab's courage didn't look like fighting in a battle. She didn't slay giants or lead armies. Her bravery was quiet, but it was powerful. She made one bold, faith-filled decision that changed the course of her life forever.

Her story reminds us:

- **Your past does not disqualify you.** No matter what others say about you—or what you've done—God sees your potential.

- **Courage starts with belief.** Even if you don't know everything about God yet, trusting Him with what you *do* know is enough to take the next step.

- **Small acts of faith can have a significant impact.** A simple cord in a window turned into a life-saving promise.

One Final Thought

Rahab didn't wait until she had everything figured out before she believed. She just started with a small thread of trust. That thread became a lifeline.

So, whether you feel like an outsider, someone with a complicated story, or just unsure of what God could do with your life, remember Rahab.

You're never too far.

You're never too small.

And you're never too late to step into something bigger.

Sometimes, all it takes is tying the cord and trusting the next chapter God is writing.

Pause & Reflect

- Is there something in your life that feels risky but right—something bold you feel called to do?

- Are there "labels" or past mistakes that you need to stop letting define you?

- What would it look like to take one small step of faith this week—even if it feels scary?

One Last Thing to Remember:

Rahab's faith didn't need a perfect past—just a willing heart. Sometimes, the boldest thing you can do is take a small step toward God and trust He'll meet you there. Your thread of belief might just be the start of your redemption story.

***

Jesus in Gethsemane: Bravery in the Face of Sacrifice

(Luke 22:39–46, Matthew 26:36–46, Mark 14:32–42)

It's late at night. The stars shimmer overhead, and the garden is quiet, still, except for the rustle of olive trees swaying in the breeze. But inside the Garden of Gethsemane, something weighty is unfolding. Jesus, fully God but also fully human, kneels alone in prayer. And what happens next gives us one of the most honest, heart-wrenching moments in all of Scripture.

He knows what's coming.

He knows that betrayal is only moments away. That pain, humiliation, and death are just around the corner. He knows the cross is near, and everything it will cost Him. And so, He prays.

"Father, if You are willing, take this cup from Me." (Luke 22:42)

This isn't a polished, picture-perfect prayer. It's raw. It's real. Jesus is in agony. The "cup" He speaks of is the suffering ahead, bearing the weight of the world's sin, facing complete separation from God. His sweat falls like drops of blood to the ground—a sign of such intense distress that even His body responds to the pressure.

But then, Jesus adds a sentence that reveals a deeper layer of courage:

"Yet not My will, but Yours be done."

In that moment, Jesus shows us what bravery truly is. It's not the absence of fear—it's the willingness to keep moving forward *despite it*. He doesn't pretend He's not hurting. He doesn't mask His anxiety. He brings it to God, fully and honestly.

That's what makes this moment so powerful.

It's not a scene of perfect calm—it's a scene of surrender. Jesus chooses God's will, even though He knows it will lead to pain. His courage isn't loud or dramatic.

It's quiet.

Submissive.

Strong.

And Then—The Betrayal

Suddenly, the stillness is broken. The crunch of feet on gravel. The flicker of torches through the trees. Soldiers appear, led by **Judas**, one of Jesus' disciples—someone who had shared meals with him, laughed with him, and called him *a friend*.

The betrayal stings. And yet, Jesus doesn't fight. He doesn't run. He doesn't panic.

He steps forward.

He allows himself to be arrested, knowing that love sometimes walks into hard places so that others might be saved—that kind of strength, peaceful, sacrificial, unwavering, unlike anything the world had seen before.

Bravery That Changed the World

At first, His closest followers scatter. Fear wins for a moment. But the memory of that night in

Gethsemane doesn't fade. The way Jesus faced the darkness, the way He submitted in trust—that memory sticks with us. And after the resurrection, His disciples began to live differently.

Peter, who once denied Jesus, now preaches with passion. Thomas, who once doubted, now believes with conviction. John, who once ran, now leads with love.

Jesus' quiet strength becomes their courage. His surrender becomes their boldness. The garden where He said yes to God becomes the spark that fuels a movement—one that still reaches us today.

What It Means for You

You may never face a moment quite like Gethsemane. However, chances are that you *have* faced moments that feel heavy—moments where you're caught between fear and faith, unsure of what to do next.

Maybe it's:

A *decision that feels overwhelming.*

A *situation that breaks your heart.*

A *call to do something brave when you'd rather stay safe.*

Whatever your moment is, **Jesus understands it**. He's been there—in the tension, in the grief, in the agony of choosing obedience over comfort.

And He shows us the way forward.

One Last Truth to Carry With You

Bravery doesn't always roar.

It often whispers through tears:

"I'm scared, but I'll stay."

"I'm hurting, but I'll keep going."

"God, I don't understand, but I trust You."

And sometimes, that quiet faith—spoken in a garden under a starry sky—is the bravest thing you'll ever do.

You don't need to have it all figured out.

You need to say yes.

Even when the night is dark and the path is painful, God's purpose is still unfolding.

And like Jesus in Gethsemane, **your yes** might become the start of someone else's hope.

Pause & Reflect

- What is your "Gethsemane" right now—where are you feeling the pressure to choose between comfort and calling?

- How can you invite God into that space with honesty, as Jesus did?

- What would it look like to say, "Not my will, but Yours"?

One Last Thing to Remember:

Jesus showed us that real bravery isn't loud—it's honest. When you're unsure or afraid, bring it to God. Even a quiet "yes" can change everything.

✳✳✳

Chapter 7 Wrap-Up: What Courage Looks Like

Courage doesn't always wear armor.

It doesn't always come with dramatic music or loud applause.

Sometimes, courage shows up in the smallest moments—the quiet ones, the hard ones, the ones no one else sees.

It's in the moment you raise your hand to speak up in class, even though your heart is racing.

It's when you decide to walk away from a situation that doesn't line up with your values, even if everyone else stays.

It's when you choose truth over popularity, peace over panic, and faith over fear.

In this chapter, we met people whose courage changed everything—not because they were fearless, but because they were faithful.

David faced a giant with nothing but a sling, stones, and trust in God.

Shadrach, Meshach, and Abednego stood firm when everyone else bowed, believing that even in the fire, God would be with them.

Jehosheba risked her life to rescue a child marked for death, proving that quiet bravery can preserve an entire future.

Joshua stepped up after Moses, led with obedience, and trusted a battle plan that made no sense—except to the God who gave it.

Rahab tied a scarlet cord in her window, believing one small act of faith could rewrite her whole story.

Jesus, in Gethsemane, said "yes" to God even when it meant deep sorrow and sacrifice. He chose love over fear—and that changed the world.

What Do All These Moments Have in Common?

They weren't easy.

They weren't perfect.

They were *brave*.

Each one required something real—**absolute trust, genuine obedience, and real courage**.

And none of them would've happened without the decision to move forward anyway, even when it was hard, scary, or uncertain.

What Courage Looks Like in Your Life

You may not be facing literal giants or fiery furnaces, but you *are* facing moments that will shape who you become.

Saying no to peer pressure.

Asking for help with something you're struggling to carry alone.

Standing up for someone who's being mistreated.

Being honest about what you believe, even if others don't understand.

Pursuing a dream that feels big—and a little scary.

And in those moments, courage means saying:

"Even if I'm afraid, I won't let fear decide for me."

"My past doesn't get to tell the whole story."

"If God is with me, I can do hard things."

One Last Thing to Hold On To:

Courage doesn't mean you never doubt or struggle; it means you face them.

It means you keep moving—even with trembling hands.

It means you stay rooted in truth when your world feels shaky.

It means you trust God's presence when the outcome isn't clear.

So, whether you're just starting your journey or standing in the middle of a battle, remember:

You were made for bravery.

Not just once but *over and over again.*

And every act of courage—no matter how small—can shift your story.

And maybe even someone else's.

Pause & Reflect

- When was the last time you chose courage over comfort?

- What "giant" are you facing that feels too big to handle on your own?

- Where is God inviting you to trust Him more, even when it feels risky?

One Last Thing to Remember:

You don't have to feel fearless to live with courage.
You just have to take the next faithful step—even when it's hard. God isn't asking for perfection. He's inviting you to trust that He's with you in every brave moment.

Looking Ahead: From Drifting to Driven

You've faced the hard questions.
You've wrestled with your identity, battled doubt, and stared down fear.

Now it's time to go deeper—to ask not just *Who am I?* but **Why am I here?**

This next chapter is all about **purpose.**

Not the pressure to have your entire life figured out, but the invitation to live with intention, right where you are.

You'll meet people who doubted they had what it takes (Jeremiah), felt too young to make a difference (Timothy), or quietly stepped into purpose with an open heart (Lydia).

You'll walk alongside a man who lived so closely with God that he didn't even taste death (Enoch) and a group of disciples who turned the world upside down—not because they were perfect, but because they were willing.

You don't have to be loud to be powerful.
You don't need a platform to have a purpose.
And you definitely don't need all the answers to take the next faithful step.

This chapter will challenge you to think bigger, live bolder, and trust that even your ordinary moments can carry extraordinary meaning.

Because your life isn't random.
It's intentional.
And you're not just here to exist.
You're here to live on purpose—with conviction, clarity, and courage.

Let's step into that calling together.

Living with Purpose and Conviction

I magine staring at a blank canvas—paintbrush in hand, heart pounding, unsure where to begin. That canvas is your life. Full of potential. Full of color. Full of questions.

What if you mess it up?

What if you're not ready?

What if no one understands what you're trying to create?

You're not alone in wondering those things. Jeremiah—the teenage prophet—felt them too.

Too Young. Too Inexperienced. Still Called.

(Jeremiah 1:4–10)

Jeremiah didn't grow up dreaming of becoming a prophet. He wasn't campaigning for attention or trying to build a platform. He was just a young man living in a hard time—a time when his nation was turning away from God, and judgment was around the corner.

Then, God showed up.

"Before I formed you in the womb, I knew you," God said. *"Before you were born, I set you apart."*

Jeremiah's response?

"I don't know how to speak. I'm too young."

Sound familiar? That feeling of I'm *not ready, I'm not enough, I can't do this?*

But God didn't argue or wait for Jeremiah to grow up. He leaned in.

"Do not say, *'I am too young.'... I am with you."*

Then God reached out, touched Jeremiah's mouth, and said,

"Now I have put my words in your mouth."

That moment wasn't about Jeremiah becoming superhuman.

It was about realizing he wasn't alone.

God didn't need him to be perfect—just *willing.*

Purpose Is Often Hard. But Always Worth It.

Jeremiah's yes didn't make his life easy.

It got *harder.*

He spoke messages that nobody wanted to hear.

He warned of destruction, begged people to turn back to God, and cried over the brokenness he saw.

He was called "the weeping prophet"—not because he was weak, but because he felt deeply.

He was misunderstood, mocked, and even thrown into a muddy pit.

His pain was real, his isolation intense. But he *kept going.* Why?

Because Jeremiah knew what he was doing mattered.

He wasn't chasing approval.

He was holding on to purpose.

And when everything else was uncertain, that purpose kept him grounded.

The Impact You Can't Always See

Not many people listened to Jeremiah at the time.

He didn't get a standing ovation or become a national hero.

But his words—faithfully written, painfully spoken—echoed across generations.

The things he said shaped history.

They became sacred scripture.

They offered hope to people in exile and courage to those waiting for restoration.

Jeremiah didn't always get to see the fruit of his obedience. But that didn't stop him from planting seeds anyway.

What Does That Mean for You?

You may not be called to be a prophet.

But you *are* called to live with purpose.

The purpose isn't always loud.

Conviction doesn't always look flashy.

And calling isn't always clear right away.

Sometimes, it means showing up for a lonely friend.

Or use your creativity to inspire someone.

Or standing for truth when it's easier to stay quiet.

Or praying for wisdom when everything feels too big.

Like Jeremiah, you don't need to wait until you "feel ready."

You need to start with a simple 'yes.'

Final Thoughts

The purpose isn't about perfection—it's about *faithfulness*.

Conviction doesn't require you to have all the answers—just the courage to keep showing up.

Whether you're painting your first strokes on the canvas of your life or adding layers to what's already begun, know this:

You matter.

Your voice matters.

And the story you're creating—stroke by brave stroke—is beautiful.

Pause & Reflect

- Have you ever felt like you were too young or too inexperienced to make a difference?

- What's one value or belief you care about deeply, and how can you live that out more boldly?

- If God is calling you toward something—even something uncertain—what might it look like to say "yes" today?

One Last Thing to Remember

You don't have to feel ready to live with purpose. Just say yes—God is already with you.

***

Timothy's Faith: Maintaining Belief in a Skeptical World

(See: Acts 16:1–5; 1 Timothy 1–6; 2 Timothy 1–4)

Timothy's story doesn't begin with fireworks or fame.

It begins in a home filled with quiet strength and lasting faith.

Long before Timothy ever preached a sermon or led a church, he was shaped by the steady influence of two women: his grandmother, Lois, and his mother, Eunice. They weren't famous, but they were faithful. They taught him the Scriptures. They showed him what it looked like to trust God day by day—even when culture didn't. Their belief ran deep, and their example planted something in Timothy that would grow into an unshakable foundation.

From Quiet Roots to Bold Purpose

When the Apostle Paul first met Timothy (Acts 16:1–2), he noticed something different.

Not just good behavior or intelligence, but *genuine faith*. Paul saw potential in Timothy and invited him to join him on his missionary journeys. That decision launched Timothy into an entirely new life, far from home, facing new cultures, new dangers, and enormous responsibility.

Timothy didn't have it easy. He was young. He was timid.

Some people dismissed him because of his age (1 Timothy 4:12).

Others tried to push false teachings, hoping he'd stay quiet or back down.

But Paul believed in him—and so did God.

Paul didn't just give Timothy assignments—he encouraged him.

In his letters, Paul poured out wisdom like a spiritual father:

- "Fan into flame the gift of God..." (*2 Timothy* 1:6)

- "Don't let anyone look down on you because you are young..." (1

Timothy 4:12)

- "Guard the good deposit that was entrusted to you..." (2 *Timothy* 1:14)

Timothy took those words to heart.

Faith That Stays Steady Under Pressure

Timothy eventually became the pastor of the church in Ephesus—one of the most influential churches in the early Christian world. His role wasn't glamorous. It wasn't easy. He faced opposition from outside the church and internal confusion as some people spread lies about Jesus. Others argued over meaningless things. Many were more interested in status than in truth.

But Timothy didn't walk away.

He stayed. He led with humility and quiet conviction.

His faith, shaped in childhood and refined by challenge, became a light amid chaos.

What made Timothy so remarkable wasn't loud charisma.

It was his consistent courage to stay rooted in what he believed, even when it wasn't popular.

What This Means for You

You might not be pastoring a church like Timothy, but you're still leading in your own way.

Maybe you're one of the only believers in your friend group.

You may be questioning your place in the faith, wondering if your doubts disqualify you from it.

Or you're trying to stay grounded in a world that keeps pulling you in different directions.

Timothy's life is proof that **you don't have to be loud to be bold.**

That **you don't have to be old to be wise.**

You **don't have to have it all together to make a lasting impact.**

Your faith doesn't need to be flashy—it needs to be *real.*

It needs to be lived out in quiet decisions:

- Saying no to gossip.

- Choosing truth when lies are easier.

- Holding onto what you know when doubts get loud.

Final Thoughts

Timothy didn't have it all figured out.

He didn't always feel brave or confident.

But he kept showing up.

He stayed rooted in what mattered most.

And because of this, he became a leader who helped shape the early church's future.

You can do the same.

When you feel pressure to fit in, remember Timothy.

When you wonder if your quiet faith is enough, remember Timothy.

When the world tells you you're too young or too soft-spoken to matter, remember Timothy.

You don't have to lead with volume.

You have to lead with truth.

Pause & Reflect

- Have you ever felt overlooked or underestimated because of your age, personality, or beliefs?

- What helps you stay grounded when your faith feels hard to hold on to?

- Is there someone in your life (like Paul was to Timothy) who encourages you to grow in faith? If not, who might you reach out to?

One Last Thing to Remember

You don't need to be loud to lead. Stay rooted in what's true, even when it's hard—quiet faith can leave a lasting mark.

***

Lydia's Influence: Making an Impact with Integrity

(*Found in Acts 16:11–15, 40*)

Imagine being a young woman today with a dream to make a difference. Perhaps you want to start a business, lead a group, create something meaningful, or be someone who stands for what's right. That same spark of purpose lived in a woman named Lydia.

She lived in the Roman city of Philippi, and she was far from ordinary. In an era when women were typically expected to stay in the background, Lydia stood out as a successful businesswoman. She sold purple cloth—a luxurious fabric reserved for royalty and the wealthy. That meant she had influence, resources, and a respected voice in her community.

But Lydia's story isn't just about money or status. It's about what she did when she heard something that touched her soul.

One day, the Apostle Paul and his friends arrived in Philippi to share the message of Jesus. They didn't have a temple or a stage. They went outside the city to a place by the river, where people gathered to pray. That's where Lydia showed up—curious, thoughtful, maybe searching for something more profound. As Paul spoke, something in his words lit a spark.

The Bible says, *"The Lord opened her heart to respond to Paul's message"* (Acts 16:14). Lydia didn't brush it off or wait for a better time. Right then and there, she made a bold decision: she believed.

She was baptized immediately—an act that demonstrated her complete commitment. And she didn't stop with herself. She brought her whole household on the journey. Her faith motivated her to act, and her first step was to offer radical hospitality. She opened her home to Paul and his team, not just as guests, but as friends, as partners in the mission. For Christians at that time, being open about their faith was risky. But Lydia didn't hide. She led with generosity and courage.

Her home became the very first church in Philippi.

Think about that: no stained glass, no pews—just a house filled with prayer, friendship, and faith. New believers gathered there to worship, encourage one another, and grow in their faith. Lydia didn't wait to be asked. She used what she had—her space, her resources, her voice—to serve. That's what authentic leadership looks like.

Lydia's story reminds us that influence doesn't require a spotlight. It comes from showing up with integrity—doing what's right, even when it's not easy or trendy. She wasn't trying to be impressive. She was trying to be faithful. And because of that, her life became a powerful part of the early church's story.

Try This: Leading Like Lydia

- Invite someone to sit with you at lunch who usually eats alone.

- Offer encouragement to someone who's trying something new.

- Utilize your creative talents (writing, art, music, or organizing) to bring people together or support a cause you care about.

You don't have to have everything figured out to make an impact. Like Lydia, you need to listen, say yes, and live what you believe—**one step, one choice, one open door at a time**.

And who knows? The small space you create might just become the place where something big begins.

Pause & Reflect

- In what areas of your life can you lead quietly—by example, through kindness, or with consistency?

- What strengths or resources do you already have that God might be inviting you to use?

One Last Thing to Remember

Leadership isn't always loud—it's faithful. When you show up with integrity and open your heart, your everyday choices can create a ripple effect that changes lives.

***

Enoch's Walk: Living Faithfully in a Faithless World

(Found in Genesis 5:21–24 & Hebrews 11:5)

You probably won't find Enoch trending online or featured in most Bible storybooks, but his life holds one of the most remarkable examples of what it means to live with quiet conviction. He didn't lead armies like Joshua, defeat giants like David, or preach to nations like Jeremiah. And yet, Enoch's story stands out for one reason: he walked with God.

That's it. That's his headline.

Genesis 5 gives us just a few verses about him:

"Enoch walked faithfully with God; then he was no more because God took him away."

(Genesis 5:24, NIV)

Wait—what? Did God take him?

Yes. According to Scripture, Enoch didn't experience death like the rest of humanity. God brought him straight into His presence. Why? Because Enoch lived a life that pleased God, not with grand performances, but with steady, faithful commitment.

What Does It Mean to "Walk with God"?

Enoch's "walk" wasn't a literal hike. It meant living in a constant relationship with God—talking to Him, listening, obeying, and aligning his everyday choices with God's heart. Enoch did this in a world that was growing darker and more self-centered by the day. This was the time leading up to Noah when people were spiraling into corruption.

But Enoch stood out, not by yelling at culture or drawing attention to himself, but by quietly choosing a different path.

He walked faithfully.

Every day, Enoch made decisions that reflected his love for God. He lived with purpose, integrity, and humility. And while we don't have the details of his daily life, we know one thing for sure: God noticed. His consistency mattered. His quiet faith carried weight.

Why Enoch Still Matters Today

Fast forward to the New Testament, and you'll find Enoch's name listed among the greats in Hebrews 11—the "Faith Hall of Fame." It says:

"By faith, Enoch was taken from this life so that he did not experience death... For before he was taken, he was commended as one who pleased God." (Hebrews 11:5, NIV)

He didn't earn awards, write bestsellers, or go viral. But he walked so closely with God that he became a living example of what faithfulness looks like.

What Enoch Teaches Us

- **Faith doesn't need to be loud to be real.**

You don't need a platform to please God. The quiet choices you make—to be kind, to be honest, to pray when no one's watching—those moments are sacred.

- **Consistency is more potent than performance.**

What you do every day, over time, speaks louder than any single bold act.

- **Your private devotion can lead to powerful transformation.**

Enoch's life encourages us to value the unseen parts of our faith journey—the quiet moments of prayer, worship, reflection, and trust.

Try This: Practice Faithfulness Like Enoch

- **Create a 7-day "Walk With God" challenge.** Spend a few minutes each day in prayer, journaling, or reading a verse of scripture. Write down one thing each day that reminds you to stay grounded in faith.

- **Pick one value**—like kindness, integrity, or humility—and live it out intentionally for a week.

- **Choose silence over noise.** Take a break from distractions (like social media) for a short time and use it to be with God.

Enoch didn't change the world by preaching to crowds. He changed it by walking faithfully with the One who made it. And that's just as needed now as it was then.

You don't need to be famous to be faithful. You don't need a spotlight to leave a legacy.

Just start walking—one faithful step at a time.

Pause & Reflect

- Are there parts of your faith that feel unnoticed or "too small" to matter?

- What would it look like to walk faithfully with God today, not just in big decisions, but in small, steady choices?

One Last Thing to Remember

A faithful life doesn't need a spotlight. God sees the quiet steps, the steady trust, and the daily walk—and in His eyes, that kind of consistency leaves a legacy.

***

The Disciples' Mission: Sharing Faith with Boldness

(*Matthew* 28:18–20, Acts 1–4)

Imagine this: you've just seen the impossible. Jesus, the one you followed, the one you saw crucified, is alive. You've walked with Him and talked with Him. Eat breakfast with Him after His resurrection. And now He's looking you in the eye, handing you a mission so big, it could change the world.

No microphones.

No big platform.

Just a simple command—and the promise of God's presence.

"Go and make disciples of all nations... And surely I am with you always, to the very end of the age." (*Matthew* 28:19–20)

This is how the movement of Christianity began—not with famous influencers or mighty armies, but with a small group of ordinary people who said *yes* to an extraordinary calling.

From Fearful to Fearless

At first, the disciples were scared. After all, they had seen their Teacher crucified. They had every reason to run and hide. Many of them did—locking themselves in a room, unsure of what came next. But Jesus didn't leave them afraid. He sent the Holy Spirit to fill them with power, courage, and boldness they never imagined.

On the day of Pentecost, flames appeared above their heads, and they began speaking languages they didn't know. So, everyone from every nation gathered in Jerusalem could understand the good news about Jesus (Acts 2). Peter, the same guy who had denied Jesus three times, stood up and preached with conviction.

Thousands believed.

That moment changed history.

But boldness didn't mean safety.

The disciples were threatened, arrested, beaten, and mocked. Still, they couldn't keep quiet. Why? Because they *knew* Jesus was alive. They had *seen* the truth, and now they were driven by it. Their courage wasn't born out of confidence in themselves—it was confidence in *God with them.*

"We cannot help speaking about what we have seen and heard." (Acts 4:20)

Try This: Boldness in Real Life

You don't have to preach to a crowd to live a life on a mission. Boldness might look like:

- Praying before lunch—even if others stare.

- Helping someone who's excluded—even if it's unpopular.

- Posting truth and encouragement on social media instead of gossip or drama.

- Inviting a friend to the youth group—even if they say no.

Boldness doesn't mean having all the answers. It means being *willing* to show up and speak up when God opens the door.

Pause & Reflect

- What's one space in your life (school, sports, friendships) where living your faith feels hard?

- What would it look like to be bold—not loud, but faithful-in that space?

One Last Thing to Remember

Bold faith doesn't mean you're fearless—it means you trust God enough to show up anyway. When you speak truth, love others, and live your faith out loud, you're continuing a mission that started with ordinary people and changed the world.

***

Jesus' Great Commission: Embracing a Lifelong Mission

(Matthew 28:18–20, See also: Acts 1:8)

Now, picture this: You're standing on a quiet hillside with your closest friends. The sky glows with early light. Jesus—your Teacher, your Savior, your Friend—is giving you one final instruction before ascending to heaven.

But this isn't a farewell—it's a launch.

A mission that doesn't end with the resurrection.

It starts right there—with you.

Jesus didn't tell His disciples to wait until they felt ready. He didn't ask for resumes, degrees, or flawless faith. He sent them—ordinary people with open hearts—to carry His message into the world.

No stage.

No spotlight.

It's just a calling.

"Go and make disciples of all nations... And surely I am with you always, to the very end of the age." (*Matthew* 28:19–20)

That moment wasn't about pressure. It was about a divine partnership where each of us had a unique role to play.

And now, you're not just a bystander; you're an integral part of the ongoing story of God's love and redemption.

Remember, you're not waiting to be sent; you're already on the mission field, making a difference in your unique way. The Great Commission isn't just for pastors or missionaries; it's for everyone. It's for everyone who believes.

Yes—even you.

Wherever you are, whatever you do—your school, your hobbies, your group chats, your team—those are your mission fields. God doesn't wait for perfect conditions to work. He works through you right where you are, whether it's in times of joy or sorrow, success or failure, comfort or discomfort.

What does that look like?

Starting a conversation about faith with a friend who's struggling.

Choosing kindness over cliques.

Using your creativity—music, sports, coding, writing—to reflect God's heart.

Forgiving when it's hard.

Inviting someone into your circle, even when it costs comfort.

You don't have to be loud. Just consistent.

You don't need to be famous. Just faithful.

Legacy of Love

The early church didn't have buildings, budgets, or celebrity pastors.

But they had love. They had each other. They had Jesus.

And they turned the world upside down.

Now it's your turn.

God placed you where you are *on purpose*. Your life, your voice, your story—it all matters.

So, take the next step.

Speak when it's uncomfortable.

Love when it's costly.

Stay faithful when it's hard.

The Great Commission isn't just an ancient instruction. It's a present invitation.

You were made for this mission.

And Jesus?

He's still with you—every step of the way.

Chapter 8 Wrap-Up: Walking in Purpose, One Step at a Time

If there's one thing Jeremiah, Timothy, Lydia, Enoch, and the disciples taught us, it's this:

You don't need to have it all figured out to live a purposeful life.

You need a willing heart and the courage to show up again and again.

Each of these individuals faced doubt, rejection, loneliness, or uncertainty. They weren't superheroes. They were human, just like you. But what set them apart wasn't perfection. It was persistence. They showed up. They listened to God. They lived with conviction.

And through those small, steady steps of obedience, they made a significant impact.

You can, too.

When you're kind to someone, no one notices.

When you speak up about what matters, even if your voice shakes.

When you choose truth over popularity.

When you stay grounded in your values, even when everything around you feels unstable.

Those moments count.

So, if you're standing at your blank canvas—uncertain, intimidated, or unsure—you're in good company. Start with one brushstroke. Take one step of faith. Trust that God is already walking with you.

The purpose isn't always loud.

Conviction doesn't always feel easy.

But when they're lived out with love, they become powerful tools for change.

You're not too young. You're not behind. You're becoming.

And God is with you in every single step.

Conclusion

Keep Building What's Unshakable

As you close this book, I want to leave you with one powerful truth:

Your faith matters.

Not someday. Not when you "have it all together." Not when you're older, louder, or more confident.

It matters right now—because God is at work in *this* moment with *your* story.

Throughout *Unshakable*, we've walked alongside:

- Jeremiah, who faced fear but still said yes.

- David, who fought with faith instead of armor.

- Esther, who risked everything to speak up.

- The disciples who shared hope with boldness.

- Lydia, who wove her faith into action.

- Shadrach, Meshach, and Abednego, who stood firm under pressure.

- Enoch, who walked faithfully in a faithless world.

- Timothy, who held fast to truth in a noisy culture.

- Rahab, who let belief lead her out of her past.

- Jesus, who faced Gethsemane with strength and surrender.

And through every story, one message has echoed:

You can live a life of unshakable faith, too.

Not because you're fearless.

Not because you never struggle.

But because you know where your foundation is.

So what's next?

- Keep asking the hard questions.

- Keep growing, even when no one's clapping.

- Keep showing up—with grace, grit, and faith.

Let scripture be your compass.

Let prayer keep you anchored.

Let the community help you rise.

Don't worry if your steps feel small. The kingdom of God is built on mustard seeds and open hands—your voice matters—your love matters. Your story matters.

God uses ordinary people to do extraordinary things.

So keep building what's unshakable:

One choice at a time.

One prayer at a time.

One brave moment at a time.

I'm honored to have walked this journey with you, and I believe with all my heart that your most excellent chapters are still ahead.

Stay strong.

Stay rooted.

Stay unshakable.

Before you close this book, take these truths with you:

- God created you with a purpose.

- You have something important to say.

- You don't need to be perfect—just willing.

- Your story isn't over yet.

- God is with you—**always.**

Let these truths be the ground beneath your feet.

You've got this.

I'm eager to see what you'll build.

Your Turn: Reflection & Response
Building Your Unshakable Faith

Take a deep breath. You've made it through stories of courage, calling, transformation, and truth. Now, it's time to reflect on *your* story.

1. What's one Bible story or person from this book that spoke to you?

Why did it stand out? How did it challenge or encourage you?

Write your thoughts here:

_____

_____

_____

2. What are the "giants" you're facing right now—fears, doubts, or challenges?

How might God be inviting you to face them with faith?

Name your giants:

_____

_____

_____

3. What does living with purpose look like for you today?

(Think: a friendship, talent, idea, or place where you feel called to show up.)

Describe it:

_____

_____

_____

4. What's one "small step" you can take this week to grow your faith?

(Pick something simple: praying before bed, inviting a friend to church, reading a Psalm, or journaling honestly.)

This week I will:

_____

_____

_____

A Prayer to Close This Chapter

"God, thank You for walking with me through every story in this book—and through every chapter of my life. Help me to live with boldness, love with purpose, and trust You when things feel unclear. I know I don't have to be perfect—I have to say yes. I want to build a faith that lasts, rooted in You. Make me unshakable. Amen."

Scan the QR code below to leave your review.

References

Youth Ministry Lesson on 1 Samuel 17: The Story of David and Goliath
https://youthgroupministry.com/lessons/youth-ministry-lesson-on-1
-samuel-17-the-story-of-david-and-goliath/

How to Listen to God's Voice: Insightful Methods for Better Communication
https://equippinghispeople.com/podcast/how-to-listen-to-gods-voic
e/

Esther: A Woman of Faith and Courage
https://www.ucg.org/good-news/good-news-magazine-november-de
cember-1996/esther-woman-faith-and-courage

Understanding Resilience from a Biblical Perspective
https://www.ibelieve.com/christian-living/understanding-resilience-f
rom-a-biblical-perspective.html

The Power of Loyalty | Lessons From Ruth's Story
https://242community.com/the-power-of-loyalty-lessons-from-ruths
-story/

Who Were Leah's Sons in the Bible – LDS Mum
https://ldsmum.com/2024/08/27/who-were-leahs-sons-in-the-bible
/

Unloved, But Overcoming! The Story of Leah
https://www.tikkunglobal.org/post/unloved-but-overcoming-the-sto
ry-of-leah

JUDAH – Faith Fellowship
https://ffmichapel.org/judah/

What Jesus Would Say to the Woman Who Has Been Raped | Bedford Alliance Church
https://bedfordalliance.church/care/abuse/what-jesus-would-say-to-the-woman-who-has-been-raped

Trauma and Belonging in the Book of Job
https://sanctuarymentalhealth.org/2023/10/26/trauma-and-belonging-in-the-book-of-job/

5 Mighty Lessons from the Miracle of Daniel in the Lion's Den
https://www.biblestudytools.com/bible-study/topical-studies/5-mighty-lessons-from-the-miracle-of-daniel-in-the-lions-den.html

Lessons from Jonah: A Bible Study About Embracing God's Plans
https://deepspirituality.com/lessons-from-jonah/

What Made Nehemiah an Effective Leader?
https://jacl.andrews.edu/what-made-nehemiah-an-effective-leader/

What Was the Relationship Between David and Jonathan?
https://www.gotquestions.org/David-and-Jonathan.html

Mary & Martha: Powerful Lessons on Faith and Priorities
https://answeredfaith.com/martha-and-mary-bible-lesson/

Abraham and Lot's Conflict – Wikipedia
https://en.wikipedia.org/wiki/Abraham_and_Lot%27s_conflict#:~:text=The%20dispute%20ends%20in%20a,continuous%20resource%20between%20two%20parties.

The Forgiveness of God: Redemption and Love
https://creativeoutreach.com/redemption-and-love/#:~:text=The%20prodigal%20son's%20journey%20begins,forgiveness%20illustrates%20God's%20boundless%20mercy.

King Solomon in the Bible: His Story and Words of Wisdom
https://www.christianity.com/wiki/people/king-solomon-in-the-bible.html

What Does Gideon Teach Us about Strong Faith?
https://www.biblestudytools.com/bible-study/topical-studies/what-does-gideon-teach-us-about-strong-faith.html

The Rich Young Ruler Reflects Our Own Struggles with Money
https://www.biblestudytools.com/bible-study/topical-studies/the
-rich-young-ruler-reflects-our-own-struggles-with-money.html#:
~:text=The%20young%20man%2C%20who%20had,enter%20the%2
0kingdom%20of%20God!

Why Did Pontius Pilate Allow Jesus to Be Crucified?
https://www.biblestudytools.com/bible-study/topical-studies/wh
y-did-pontius-pilate-allow-jesus-to-be-crucified.html

Understanding the Good Samaritan Parable
https://www.biblicalarchaeology.org/daily/archaeology-today/arc
haeologists-biblical-scholars-works/understanding-the-good-sam
aritan-parable/

Book of Esther – Wikipedia
https://en.wikipedia.org/wiki/Book_of_Esther#:~:text=The%20st
ory%20takes%20place%20during,chosen%20as%20the%20new%20
queen.

Amos' Call for Social Justice in Amos 5:21-24
http://www.scielo.org.za/scielo.php?script=sci_arttext&pid=S1010
-99192021000200005#:~:text=In%20the%20verse%2C%20the%20
message,humanhuman%20relationship%20and%20human%2DGod

Tax Collectors and Sinners
https://bibleodyssey.net/articles/tax-collectors-and-sinners/

The Conversion of Paul and Its Impact on Christianity
https://faithhub.net/the-conversion-of-paul-and-its-impact-on-c
hristianity/

4 Lessons from Jacob's Ladder to Encourage and Challenge You
https://www.crosswalk.com/faith/bible-study/lessons-from-jaco
bs-ladder-to-encourage-and-challenge-you.html

**John 4:1-30, 39-42 – The Woman at the Well: A Community
Transformed**
https://www.susanvillemethodist.org/pastorsblog/john-41-30-39-
42-the-woman-at-the-well-a-community-transformed

Encounters with Christ: Peter's Reinstatement
https://shereadstruth.com/encounters-with-christ-peters-reinstatem
ent/

David and Goliath – 1 Samuel 17 (Bible Lessons for Teens)
http://truewaykids.com/david-and-goliath-teen/

Unyielding Faith: The Courage of Shadrach, Meshach, and Abednego
https://medium.com/@DailyDevotionals/unyielding-faith-6b2e53ecdd
3c

Genuine Faith – Living Word Ministries (Audio Archive)
https://bottradionetwork.com/ministry/living-word-ministries/2022-
10-02-genuine-faith/

7 Powerful Lessons from the Fall of the Walls of Jericho
https://www.biblestudytools.com/bible-study/topical-studies/power
ful-lessons-from-the-fall-of-the-walls-of-jericho.html

The Life and Faith of the Prophet Jeremiah
https://frkevinkilgore.com/2022/04/08/the-life-and-faith-of-the-pr
ophet-jeremiah/

Saint Timothy – Wikipedia
https://en.wikipedia.org/wiki/Saint_Timothy#:~:text=Timothy%20be
came%20St%20Paul's%20disciple,on%20their%20journey%20to%20M
acedonia.

Lydia of Thyatira: The Founding Member of the Philippian Church
https://margmowczko.com/lydia-of-thyatira-philippi/

Enoch Bible Study: Walking with God (Genesis 5; Hebrews 11)
https://activechristianity.org/enoch-bible-study-walking-with-god-ge
nesis-5-hebrews-11

www.ingramcontent.com/pod-product-compliance
Lightning Source LLC
Chambersburg PA
CBHW061745120626
46550CB00005B/1892